UNTIL I HAVE NO COUNTRY

A Novel of King Philip's War in New England

Michael J. Tougias

M J Tougias

COVERED BRIDGE PRESS

North Attleborough, Massachusetts

To the Algonkian People of New England.
And to my parents. Arthur gave me his passion for history,
and Jerri her love of novels.

ISBN 0-924771-80-1

10 9 8 7 6 5

Covered Bridge Press
North Attleboro MA

Author's Note

King Philip's War was fought between the Native Americans and the early colonial settlers of New England in 1675–76. In per capita terms, this war was the bloodiest conflict in America's history, and it helped shape the white man's tendency toward military solutions whenever settlers moved into tribal lands.

At the center of the cataclysm was one man, Metacom, leader of the Pokanokets, a tribe within the Wampanoag Indian Federation. At an early age, when relations between natives and settlers were less stressed, Metacom was given the name of Philip by the English, a name he used (among others) even during the war.

One of the many ironies of this conflict is that Philip was the son of Massasoit—the same Massasoit who helped the Pilgrims survive their first winter in the New World. A father's kindness became a son's curse.

In the 55-year span between the arrival of the Mayflower and the outbreak of the war, the English prospered, multiplied and expanded their settlements, while the natives were in a slow state of decline from disease (introduced by the Europeans) and loss of tribal lands to the whites.

By 1675 the stage was set for conflict, and it was Philip who stepped forward, recognizing that his people would have no country if the trend continued.

Historians might argue Philip's importance in the war, and it's true that other sachems commanded more warriors. But it was Philip's braves who started the war, and it was Philip who criss-crossed the region in an effort to unite the other tribes. He was a man of courage and vision.

Until I Have No Country is the story of Tamoset, a friend of Philip, who was thrust into the eye of the storm.

Real Life Characters

Although some of the primary characters in this book are fictional, the following people all lived during the time of King Philip's War and were significantly involved:

English Characters	*Native Americans*
Benjamin Church	Awashonks
Captain Gardner	Canonchet
Lieutenant Holyoke	Muttawump
Captain Lothrop	Philip
Captain Moseley	Weetamoo
Mary Rowlandson	
Captain Turner	
Roger Williams	
General Winslow	

Prologue

June 1675

Tamoset was sitting by the bay in the pre-dawn hours when the vision came. Suddenly the bay disappeared, and he was looking down from a hilltop into a river valley he had never seen before. Thick blue-grey smoke rose from scattered clearings in the forest below. It spread like fog and mingled with the orange sky above. He knew the smoke came from white men's farms that were burning. Mesmerized, he watched as the forest closed in on the clearings, swallowing them up as if they had never existed. He wondered if the Great Creator would speak to him, and he waited, hoping.

Time passed, and the strange valley changed. First the colors of autumn spread over the forest, followed by the harsh winter landscape covered in snow. A white owl floated by, and he shuddered as the bird looked directly at him. He was filled with dread and gloom, and he tried to close his eyes to escape the scenes. But his eyes would not close, nor could he move his body. Only when he saw the river turn red with blood--his people's blood--did the images stop.

His heart was pounding as the bay came back into focus, shimmering under the moonlight. He was shaken to the core and drenched in sweat. So this is why I could not sleep, he thought, I needed to see this. But what did it mean? Nothing like this had ever happened to him before, and he wondered what he should do. He knew he could not tell his wife, for she was frightened enough by the recent talk of war.

Now the sweat chilled him, and he stood up, turning his back on the bay to return to the sleeping village. Already he was doubting what he had seen. Maybe the blood was not of our people, he thought, maybe it was English blood. He decided to tell no one.

* * * *

The night that Tamoset had his vision, two young boys slipped out of the village, and ran northward. Four miles later they stopped and hid in vegetation where huge trees met a field with a cabin in its center. Here, they patiently waited for darkness to be replaced by the light of grey dawn. Each held a bow in his hands already notched with an arrow.

The bigger boy, the leader of the two, nudged the other when a pale light appeared from the cabin's tiny window.

"English sleep late," he said with a smile.

"He is lazy, his cattle-house is not finished and he rests until the eastern sky is pink," joked the other boy.

Now that the mist was breaking up, they had their first look inside the clearing. The house was very small, with a steeply pitched roof. Through the window they saw the dark outline of the white man's head. Next to the house was a small barn, with only the frame of the roof completed. Fresh cut logs lay scattered about.

Now smoke began to rise from the stone chimney of the crude dwelling.

"Why does he build such a big fire in the growing season?"

The bigger boy shook his head, "Maybe he thinks it is going to snow, maybe he thinks it scares away wolves and ... ."

Both boys froze as the cabin door opened. Their eyes widened when they saw the blond hair on the man. They had only seen two other whites before, the two that came to talk to Philip, their tribe's sachem, but both of those men had black hair like themselves.

Picking up a switch that leaned against the cabin, the white man walked to the barn and removed the plank that held the door shut. Inside, the cattle bawled, impatient to feed. Once the farmer had the door opened, the cattle left the barn on their own, fanning out through the small clearing, eager to pick at the bits of green in the rocky field.

The man walked to the pile of logs, lifting his axe to begin the day's work. He was no more than thirty yards from the young braves.

Slowly the boys pulled back on their bowstrings, and let their arrows fly.

* * * *

When they returned to the village, their fathers were waiting. The boys were astonished. They thought they had slipped out of their wigwams without a sound in the middle of the night, assuming their parents would think them hunting when they awoke.

"Where have you been?"

The bigger boy addressed his father as calmly as he could, "The ducks are thick on the tidal pools, we ... ."

"Do not lie. One does not go north to kill ducks."

Silence, the boy's mind racing. To continue to lie now would be unthinkable.

"We went to where the Englishman is building on our land." He paused, voice shaking. "I heard you talking about him, saying he should be dealt with. We wanted to help the tribe."

His father clenched his teeth, the only outward sign of his rage. "Talk more."

"We killed two of his cattle. We did not harm the man. We ... we wanted to scare him away."

The two fathers looked at each other, shaking their heads. They moved out of earshot from the boys and talked briefly. When they returned, the one who had spoken before said, "We will tell Philip. Now."

They found their leader outside his wigwam, playing with his son. Philip was an impressive figure: tall, well-muscled, with piercing black eyes set above a hooked nose. Those that knew him said you could read his thoughts through his eyes, that in one quick look he could make you feel like an old friend or send a shiver down your spine.

Philip stood, sending his son inside the wigwam, and then set his gaze on the men, knowing something had happened for them to come to him so early in the day.

The men explained what their sons had done, then stood silently.

Philip looked at the two fathers, then down at the boys, who were visibly shaking. He motioned for the boys to leave, and they ran, leaving their fathers to face the sachem alone.

Fingering a stone amulet carved with a wolf's head that hung from his neck, Philip turned his gaze to the bay. His expression was blank, but one of the men noticed he was clenching his teeth, jaw muscle showing taut through copper-colored skin.

A minute passed, then Philip addressed the men. "The boys should not have killed the cattle. But there will be no punishment. The English must learn not to build their square houses on disputed land."

He abruptly turned away, thinking that the time had come to let his people decide what to do about the whites.

Indian Villages and Colonial Settlements
~ King Philip's War 1675-76 ~

Great River Camp

Wachusett Camp

Deerfield

Nipmuck Land

Nipmuck Village

Brookfield

BOSTON

Connecticut River

Springfield

Medfield

Plymouth

Wampanoag Land

Hartford

Montaup Village (Mt. Hope)

Providence

Pocasset Swamp Camp

Narragansett Land

Great Swamp Camp

N

Atlantic Ocean

Chapter 1

The rhythm of running was like music to Tamoset. That was his secret. He knew that physical powers were enhanced when the spirit was in harmony with the body, allowing him to run faster and farther than the other braves of the tribe.

He felt that power now as he raced along the green woodland path headed back to his village at Montaup. He could hear the light patter of Ponotuck's moccasins keeping pace behind him. Ponotuck was a great runner in his own right, and for this reason he was told to assist Tamoset on this important journey.

It was three days since the boys killed the cattle, but it seemed much longer to Tamoset. Philip had called a hasty council then sent Tamoset and Ponotuck on a mission to enlist the support of the Narragansetts should war break out with the English. Now the two braves were racing back to Philip with the Narragansett decision.

Beads of sweat dripped down Tamoset's forehead and into his eyes, but he didn't feel the sting. He was aware of every forest sound, alert for any movement, yet his mind was free to roam. Just now he was thinking of Philip. Will I forever be following him? Will I ever be able to say no?

Tamoset knew the answer to his own question. He was trapped by duty—a tribal duty stronger than his own family. Philip always appealed to the sense of honor, his words striking just the right chords in the listener. Philip's real power was in persuasion. That's why he was sachem of the Wampanoag tribe.

Tamoset let his thoughts drift back to the words of the council Philip held. He was among the select group of warriors and elders that had gathered in the large wigwam called a long house. The men formed a double ring around a small fire that cast dancing light on anxious faces. They had not been told why they were gathered, but most thought that Philip would discuss the action of the boys that killed the cattle. Maybe he would warn them to control their children—or face his wrath.

Philip was seated with them, letting the tension mount as the pipe was passed. His long black hair was pulled back tight, eyes glowing in the firelight. Around his waist was a snakeskin belt with tiny, polished shells woven into it.

When the clay pipe completed its circle and returned to the sachem, he took a long, leisurely draw, as if he were alone by his cooking fire. Then, in a deep, calm voice, he began.

"I wish to talk of a grave matter, and to do so I must start at the beginning of our troubles. Massasoit spent many hours telling me about the early days."

Those gathered now knew for certain this was more than an ordinary council because Philip rarely discussed his father.

He continued slowly, "The English would have starved during those early years, had it not been for our kindness. My father felt pity for them. We gave them our corn, we gave them our fish. We taught them how to hunt the deer, turkey and partridge. We showed them how to plant beans, pumpkin, squash and corn. That was many seasons ago. They prospered and have long since forgotten our friendship. We gave, and what did they do? They took our lands and favorite hunting grounds, saying that words on paper allowed them to do so. Now they harbor dark suspicions against us."

Philip paused to let the council absorb his words. Like any strong leader, his speaking skills were considerable. He knew that to gain full support he must build his case. All eyes were on him as he cleared his throat to continue.

"You all remember how the English came and took my brother, Alexander, away from his family and marched him to Plymouth. He never returned. The English would have us believe he became ill, but we know he was strong like the bear. No, Alexander was poisoned for being a leader. Next they will be coming to take me. They say I am a threat."

The crackle of the ceremonial fire was the only sound in the long house. Tamoset sat perfectly still. What Philip said was true, and years of frustration had now reached the boiling point. Normally a thoughtful and objective person, Tamoset found himself struggling to contain his emotions. Although Philip had never once raised his voice, all the men had been worked into a burning rage.

The men looked to Philip to continue, the silence growing awkward. Instead he took his time, staring into each man's eyes, trying to read what was in their hearts. Finally, he opened his palms, the signal that the others may speak.

An elder cleared his throat and put down his pipe, saying, "My seasons left in this world are but few. I would like to enjoy my grandchildren, share my knowledge, then die in peace. But I am Wampanoag, and a Wampanoag does not sit idly by as his sachem is taken by the strangers. I may be white on the head, but I can still fight."

The others nodded, murmuring in agreement. The old man in his wisdom and simplicity had spoken for the pride in all of them.

Philip knew he had them. Now was the time to make them think it was their idea. Let them complete the plan. He spoke once more.

"We must consider the consequences of our actions. If we take to the warpath, all the whites in the country will come for us. The Wampanoags alone are no match for the hordes of whites. Remember what they did to the Pequots long ago."

Again silence. One of the braves could no longer hold his tongue, saying, "That may be true, but I can no longer live like a prisoner with the strangers closing in. We must find a way to fight and win!"

The men erupted, shouting, "war, war, war!"

Philip put his hand up for silence, waiting for the outburst to subside.

"I have lain awake many nights thinking of this. There must be others who think as we do. Surely other tribes are also losing their land. And if you lose your land, you cannot feed your family, and even the most peace-loving will fight for his woman and children. We have never had good relations with the other tribes, but we have never faced a common enemy. We must go to them and seek to unite. Now is the time."

This gave the council much hope, and they discussed which tribes they would approach first and who would carry the message. Then they all smoked the pipe as a symbol of unity.

Some were wildly happy at the decision, while others, primarily the older ones, were uncertain. But they too eventually supported the plan. They could see no options: the Massachusetts Bay Colonists were expanding to their north, the Plymouth Colonists were encroaching from the east, and the Nipmucks and Narragansetts controlled the land to the south and west.

Philip rose to close the council. Standing at the center of the ring, next to the glowing fire, he said: "I have told the whites at Providence and now I will tell you: I am determined not to live until I have no country."

* * * *

But now, after council with the Narragansetts, Tamoset knew Philip was wrong. The Narragansetts would not join them in war against the English, and without them there was little hope of success. And he could not forget the vision —it was a bad omen, a warning. He must tell Philip, stop him from the warpath until the time was right.

Tamoset motioned for Ponotuck to stop running. Evening's light was almost gone, and the braves had been on the move all day, covering well over thirty miles. They were now in a forest that neither the Wampanoags nor the Narragansetts lay claim to, yet both tribes hunted there. Tamoset did not think it wise to run in the dark. If they surprised a Narragansett hunting party they might be viewed as hostile, and the arrows would fly before their was time to talk.

They stopped at the shore of a small pond fed by a trickle of water bouncing down from a hillside spring. Both men got down on hands and knees and drank deeply from the stream.

The taste of cool, sweet water was enhanced by the dank earth smells rising from the ferns which grew in the well-shaded forest.

When they had drunk their fill, they stood up and walked to the pond's edge, looking out over its black waters in the fading light. Ponotuck was tall and slender; his graceful body had earned him the nickname "fox," while Tamoset was built more like a small bear. Their light, tawny-colored skin was remarkably smooth and clear.

Ponotuck wore his hair in a long single braid with a brightly colored headband stretched across his forehead. Tamoset preferred the style his father had worn—his scalp was plucked on the sides, and only a short strip of hair ran down the middle of his head, which he kept stiff with grease and paint. Other tribe members plucked their heads on one side and let the hair grow long on the other.

Tamoset stared at the tops of the trees that ringed the pond. June's full foliage extended from the ground to the sky. The dark, sweeping branches of enormous hemlocks gave the pond an enchanting quality. Did the trees know that the settlers were coming with their axes, Tamoset wondered? It was painful for him to consider that these stately giants might be cut; each tree had its purpose and was part of the whole.

Ponotuck was thinking of the council with Canonchet, the sachem of the Narragansetts. Even without the Narragansetts, he wanted to fight the English, relishing the thought of winning honor in battle. He turned to Tamoset. "Not all the Narragansett braves will follow Canonchet, some will fight."

"You are wrong. He is their sachem," said Tamoset, "they will honor him."

"Maybe. But later, when they hear of our battles, the younger braves will come and join us."

Tamoset frowned. "There will be no fighting, the time is not right."

"Philip will decide that. And he is not slow like the turtle first leaving the mud in the spring. He has waited long enough. You heard him at the council. If he cannot convince Canonchet to join us, he will go to the Nipmucks. If they say no, he will go to the Pocumtucks. If he must, he will fight alone, and so will I."

Tamoset decided not to respond. He had been friends with Ponotuck for years, and decided to ignore the hint of an insult. He knew Ponotuck was impatient, knew he was tired of seeing the whites get stronger.

Tamoset turned toward a grove of pine trees and said, "We will sleep here and run at first light."

No fire was built; the men simply ate the ground corn they carried, re-greased their hair and bodies, and laid down on the ferns they piled over the pine and hemlock needles.

Before falling asleep Tamoset thought of his wife, Napatoo, and baby son. Napatoo had begged him not to make this mission, arguing that it was much too dangerous, and that he was needed for the summer hunting.

"Now that we have a baby," she reasoned, "you should be with your family. Philip is using you, he always has, I know how his mind works."

Few men loved their wives more than Tamoset loved Napatoo, and his elation over the birth of his son, Chusett, knew no bounds. But Tamoset could not turn his back on Philip, and so his parting with Napatoo had been a quiet one. She prepared his pouch of cornmeal, but there was no goodbye.

What would war mean for his family? Tamoset had never been at war before; in fact, he had never killed another man. He could not begin to fathom all the consequences of fighting the English, yet instinctively he knew that those optimistic young braves who thought they would drive the English back across the Great Water were wrong. The English were firmly entrenched in towns such as Boston, Plymouth and Providence.

At least, he thought, war meant the possibility of revenge. Tamoset's father had died from the Sickness, as had thousands of other Indians. Tamoset had heard stories of this plague, and it was said over half his tribe had suffered and died from it. The Sickness was also sarcastically referred to as the white man's "gift" because the disease was brought by the first white explorers. The elders of the Wampanoag tribe often talked of the days before the ships arrived, when almost every Indian lived out his or her full natural cycle and only the very young or the very old got sick. But his father had died in the prime of life.

Tamoset fell asleep thinking of his father and dreamed he was nine years old again. They were hunting together on the edge of a marsh near Montaup. It was autumn and the gold marsh grass was framed by a tree line of yellow, crimson and orange. The young boy was filled with happiness; he was with his father, and both felt the power and joy of the Great Spirit as they walked along a trail.

The dream suddenly turned into a nightmare when his father yelled, "Run, Tamoset, run!" Then thunder came in a deafening roar. The boy turned to hug his father in fear, but instead saw a bloody corpse where he had been standing. From the woods there emerged screaming white soldiers, each one armed with an enormous musket. Behind the soldiers came the farmers and their wives, whose faces were contorted with a manic rage. Each farmer carried a pitchfork. Soldiers and farmers made a ring around the terrified boy. The muskets were pointed directly at him. And then they all fired at once.

Tamoset's whole body jerked, and he woke with a start. He looked over at Ponotuck, but the brave was sleeping soundly. "What's happening to me?" he asked himself, "First the vision and now this dream." Then he looked up through the pines and gazed at the stars, wondering if his father was watching. There would be no sleeping the rest of the night.

* * * *

At dawn, they started running again. Tamoset had not uttered a word all morning, and Ponotuck knew better than to ask him what was wrong.

The run back to Montaup seemed to take forever. A light rain fell as the two braves neared the village outskirts in the late afternoon. Gray mist settled over the hills, mirroring Tamoset's troubled thoughts. It was critical to warn Philip that it was too early for war. To attack, without the aid of the Narragansetts or other tribes, would be disastrous.

Still a half mile from the village center, they were surprised when five Indians streaked with war paint suddenly jumped out of the bushes. The painted warriors immediately recognized their fellow tribesmen and cheered wildly.

The tallest of the warriors made himself heard above the rest, shouting, "It has started, we have killed the whites at Swanzey!"

Tamoset was stunned. A sickening feeling spread over him. He knew the killing would come sooner or later, but he always thought it would be later. And here I am, he thought, trying to warn Philip that the time is not right.

The warriors went on with their recounting of the day's events. One of them raised his fist, yelling, "They fired the first shot. We killed nine farmers; the others are fleeing to the east!"

Tamoset heard enough. His thoughts were on Napatoo and the baby, little Chusett. This early blood-letting was a bad omen. A twinge of guilt made him feel worse. I'm partly responsible, he thought. I could have urged for more deliberation at Philip's council, but instead I was as swept up in war talk as the others. Now, after years of threats, it was actually happening.

Motioning for Ponotuck to follow, he began sprinting toward the village, leaving the warriors to continue boasting on their own.

* * * *

Tamoset's first duty was to locate Philip. He found him at the main lodge, preparing to go to the field to instruct the braves. Black paint covered one side of his face, and red on the other.

"Philip!" Tamoset cried, "We must stop this madness; the Narragansetts will not join us."

Philip gripped his friend by both shoulders, and leveled piercing black eyes at him. He was calm.

"It is too late, the arrow has left the bow. Others will join us when they see our courage. But now, like the great bear, we must fight alone. I think the whites will come for us in two or three days, so we must prepare an ambush."

"But ..."

Philip shook his head, indicating the decision was final. "We are doing the right thing."

And with those words said, Philip trotted out of camp with three other tribal leaders. He looked back at Tamoset and shouted, "We will talk later, I will be back soon!"

Tamoset's mind raced. Too much was happening at once. He watched Philip go and then ran toward home.

Exhausted and drenched with rain and sweat, he burst into his family wigwam. It took a moment for his eyes to become accustomed to the dim light. Napatoo sat quietly at the rear of the hut, nursing Chusett. She put her hand up in a gesture of silence and gave Tamoset a sad smile.

Napatoo adored her husband and felt an enormous sense of relief upon seeing him back safely. She had been on edge since he left, and felt bad about the cold way she had treated him. And today had been a nightmare, with rumors of all-out war and fear of soldiers charging the village. Now, with Tamoset home, she allowed herself to relax. Together, they would face the trouble.

As the baby fed, Napatoo stared at her husband, taking in the haggard look of his face, but noting how his eyes shone with concern and love. It was Tamoset's eyes that had first attracted Napatoo when they met four years ago. They reflected a sensitive man, a thoughtful man.

When the baby had drunk himself full, she placed him in the woven basket where he slept. The child put two fingers in his mouth and within seconds was fast asleep. Now she turned her gaze back to Tamoset. She noticed he was staring at her breasts, and that made her smile.

"I missed you," she whispered, pulling him toward the bed mat, "Come lie with me."

He started to speak, but Napatoo shook her head. "We have tomorrow to talk."

Tamoset lay beside her, holding her tightly. The harsh feelings of the past night were forgotten. Later, with the patter of falling rain providing their drum beat, they slowly made love.

Chapter 2

A small shaft of dim light, shining through the wigwam's opening, awakened Tamoset. For a few seconds he rested peacefully, in the groggy, comfortable period when the mind has not yet kicked into full activity. But then the events of yesterday came rolling into consciousness like thunder, causing him to shake his head, as if it was a bad dream he might escape.

Quelling the impulse to rush to Philip and the other warriors, he turned and looked at Napatoo. She lay sleeping on her side facing him, her long glossy black hair spread over the reed mat. Slight of build, and only twenty, she still had a delicate, almost child-like appearance. He was glad that slumber had replaced her worried look of yesterday with an expression of utter tranquility.

Now, he reached out and ran his hand down along the soft skin of her side, wondering if they would ever have another morning like this. When she did not respond he did it again, this time slowing his finger tips as they crossed over her belly and onto her thigh.

Her eyelids fluttered but did not open. I'll let her sleep a few more minutes, he thought, it will be a difficult day. He propped his head up on one elbow, watching her, thinking how beautiful she was, how smooth her skin. She was everything he desired in a wife, and he still felt lucky she chose him.

In his earlier years he had felt uncomfortable around women, like a deer in open country, and used to watch Napatoo from afar. His shyness prevented him from talking to her, or to any of the other young women in the village.

Growing up with Philip and Ponotuck, he had plenty of opportunities to observe the ease with which the two of them dealt with the opposite sex. At times they pretended not to notice the girls of the village, but on other occasions they joked and laughed with them, while Tamoset stood in the background.

Ponotuck, bragging and teasing at the same time, always had girls around him, always with a smile. Philip was not as accessible and was often indifferent to the girls that showered him with attention. Even in his teens Philip commanded special attention, exuding a power and confidence beyond his years, and this attracted the opposite sex.

It was Philip who first became interested in Napatoo, and for a time it looked like they might marry. But inexplicably the budding romance ended. Months went by, and Napatoo kept her distance from Philip, which meant Tamoset rarely saw her as well.

On the few occasions that Napatoo and Tamoset did pass each other in the village, she smiled, always with a light and happy air about her. Tamoset became infatuated with her, but could never muster more than a few words of greeting. A whole year went by before conversation between the two evolved from pleasantries to more serious discussions.

It was then that Napatoo saw the depth of the man, and was amazed that the two of them shared the same feelings about certain members of the tribe. They sought out each other's company more and more, talking about everything—except Philip. Whatever had happened between them would remain a mystery, and Tamoset had no intention of asking. He was happy just to be with her, and it seemed Philip was glad for him as well.

Now, he knew their life was going to change. Just how much, and for how long, he had no idea, but he knew the killing of the whites would somehow affect every single member of the tribe. He didn't want to break the mood of the morning, didn't want to worry her, but knew he must tell her his plans. Stroking her hair, she slowly awoke.

"Napatoo, we must talk," he whispered.

She opened her eyes, was about to smile, but stopped when she saw the serious look on his face. Then she remembered the killing of the whites.

Tamoset took her hand. "Today I must join Philip in the field. Sooner or later the whites will be coming."

She stared at him for a moment, before sighing and asking, "What about Chusett and I?"

"I'm not sure, but I think it best to pack our things. I'll be back soon."

Napatoo held her tongue, wanting to choose her words carefully to avoid an argument. She too sensed that negotiation with the whites was impossible now. There would be bloodshed, and she hoped all would then see the futility of fighting. Inside she was still angry; just when her life finally seemed complete, Philip was ruining it with his plans of war. She had dreamed of having a large family with Tamoset, wanted nothing more than to spend her days with him, Chusett and the children to follow. Now that would have to wait.

She knew Tamoset had his doubts about the war, and thought that this might be her last chance to make him reconsider.

Taking hold of his hand, she rolled to her back. She did not look at him, but instead kept her eyes on the wigwam's blackened smoke hole, now covered for the warm season. She spoke in a soft voice, as if to herself.

"We kill some of them, they kill some of us. Where will it lead? I hate them as much as you do, but this is not the way. I know you want revenge for the death of your father. And I know Philip's words have the power of a river running in the springtime. But I also think you have your doubts. You feel you have no other course, but you do—we do. We could go to Awashonk's tribe and stay there until this storm of killing passes."

Tamoset put his arm around her, and shook his head slowly. "Too late for that; we will do best if the tribe sticks together. I know you want Chusett safe—you are a good mother, and what you say are the words of a mother trying to protect her family. But there is no real safety now."

She did not get angry, but a great sadness filled her. She understood he could not leave the tribe, and for that matter, she wasn't even sure that she could either. Maybe the Great Creator will guide us, she thought; he has always favored Tamoset. I will not trouble him again with such talk.

She pulled him close. Outside a dog barked and the village slowly came awake. She knew this might be the last day she had him by her side for many moons, and she wanted it to last as long as possible. She nuzzled her head into his shoulder, breathing deeply of his scent while letting her hands explore his body.

Tamoset was becoming aroused and went to kiss her, but suddenly there were shouts coming from outside.

He scrambled up and ran out. Fog hung to the ground and Tamoset raced after other villagers toward the sound of voices. Then, through the grayness he saw many people gathered about a scout, and heard the word "soldiers."

He muscled his way through the crowd. "From which direction?" he demanded of the scout.

"They come on the Plymouth Trail," the brave answered, pointing toward the northeast. "An ambush has been set if they go past Swanzey."

People started talking excitedly amongst themselves while the village elders peppered the scout with questions. Now that Philip was in the field, there was no one leader in charge, and decisions would be made by consensus. Many of the tribe's more influential women were for an immediate evacuation of the village. Montaup sat at the end of a peninsula that jutted into Narragansett Bay, and the women argued that they might be trapped.

Tamoset discussed the situation with the elders. Most, including Tamoset, advocated a wait-and-see approach. Montaup had been their tribal seat for as long as anyone could remember, and abandoning it ran counter to their nature. Besides, the soldiers were still several miles away, and Philip, along with most of the warriors, would know exactly where they were.

Tamoset returned to the wigwam. Napatoo had already started packing. Chusett was awake in the basket.

"Tamoset," she said in a hushed voice, "you can't go to Philip now; we need you here."

He paused, could see the strain in her face. "Yes, I will stay for now; there are very few men here."

Napatoo picked up Chusett and held him tightly. "The English have come so quickly."

"I thought we would have more time. But I should have known they would come immediately. What did we expect would happen when we kill so many whites in Swanzey?"

* * * *

Tamoset helped Napatoo pack furs, tools, cooking utensils, bowls and dried food. In less than an hour almost everything was bundled into three large baskets, and he left to meet with the elders.

No sooner did he arrive at the council lodge than another runner burst into the village, reporting that an even larger group of soldiers had been seen marching rapidly down the Northeast Path. Everyone knew these men were coming from Boston. The Wampanoags had incurred the wrath not only of Plymouth Colony, but also of the larger Massachusetts Bay Colony as well.

As word spread through the village, near panic erupted. Mothers screamed for their children, and dogs, caught up in the excitement, barked wildly. Dust rose as people ran from wigwam to wigwam, while others went to tell those who were tending the crops.

There was no argument this time over what to do: all understood that to stay on Montaup, with such a large army approaching, could mean slaughter. Confusion, however, had taken hold of the village, as people argued over escape routes.

Three elder men approached Tamoset and asked that he lead the exodus from the village.

"No," said Tamoset firmly, "choose someone else."

"The people need you. And the Great Creator has you here at the village for this reason," said one of the elders sharply. He put his hand on Tamoset's arm. "The Spirit brought you back safely to the village, knowing we would be in crisis."

Tamoset looked at their lined and weathered faces, men he had known since boyhood, each a friend of his father's. They, in turn, were staring back at him with stern, stoic looks, their emotions hidden. To refuse their request, which was now an order, was impossible.

Tamoset nodded. At least he knew where they should go; there was only one place where women and children would be safe.

"Tell the people that when the sun is directly overhead, all villagers must be packed. Have them assemble at the shore. Send runners to Philip; tell him we are leaving for the Pocasset Swamp."

Knowing someone was in charge had a calming affect on the village, and the desertion of Montaup went smoothly. Dugout canoes first took the women and children eastward across the narrow bay. Next the elders went. Once these villagers were safely out, the boys who were left behind, being too young for the warpath, were put to work shuttling both personal and communal property across the choppy waters.

Few villagers noticed that the baskets of dried cornmeal from the prior season's crops had dwindled to no more than a dozen. This year's crops were a long way from harvest, but their precious fields had to be abandoned.

Although the move transpired efficiently, the uneasy feeling continued. Children asked why they were leaving home. Mothers nervously answered that they were going to a neighboring tribe's celebration, but their eyes constantly scanned the woods for signs of the enemy.

When the last canoe-load of belongings had crossed the bay, Tamoset and Napatoo led the way along a trail that snaked towards Pocasset Swamp. The English hated and feared swamps, referring to them as the devil's den and a place of darkness. Tamoset had heard about that fear and knew the whites would be reluctant to follow.

To the east, where the majority of English had settled, Tamoset had watched from afar as the farmers struggled to rid their towns of wetlands. As soon as the settlers had erected their houses, they began digging ditches to drain the swamps and marshes so that the cattle could graze on the rich grasses.

To the Wampanoags, swamps were known as the givers of life. Certain healing herbs and roots could be found only in the flooded areas. Food of all sorts grew in abundance, especially waterfowl. The arrival of springtime meant the return of migratory ducks, and ceremonies were held for the hunters, with the villagers counting the days until they could once again enjoy the the taste of roast duckling. Deer and bear were hunted from the silence of a canoe, while muskrat lodges were raided for the many succulent tubers cached there. And now the swamp would act as a hiding place.

The day was sultry, the fog had long since burned off, and the walk on the winding trail was long and difficult as everyone labored under the burden of their baskets and packs of belongings. At sundown they set up camp on a small island surrounded by shallow water. Anyone trying to reach them would have to pass through a jungle-like growth of black spruce, red maple, oak, and a thick tangle of low-lying vegetation.

* * * *

The next day, Tamoset learned that the villagers had escaped just in the nick of time—a large force of soldiers had arrived at Montaup, burning wigwams, trampling crops and then erecting a fort for themselves.

Philip was like an enraged bull, and he attacked the nearby towns of Dartmouth and Middleboro, leaving ashes and blood in his wake. But more soldiers arrived at Montaup over the next few days, engaging the warriors in brief but pitched skirmishes, some not far from where Tamoset had hidden the families.

Chapter 3

"Philip is coming tomorrow, and I'll talk with him about what to do next," said Tamoset. He began preparing a cooking fire in front of the little wigwam they had erected in the swamp camp. "But first I must go off alone and hear the silence before I offer counsel."

Napatoo sat cross-legged with the baby sleeping in her lap. She pulled stems from the wild strawberries and blackberries they had gathered. Looking up, she spoke what had been in her mind since they arrived. "Philip will only listen to words of war, not peace."

Reaching out for Tamoset's hand, she continued, "Tamoset, please talk of peace. If Philip won't listen to you, let's leave this place. I want Chusett to be as far away from Philip and the English as possible."

He squeezed her hand. "Everything will be all right. We can't stay here forever. We need to grow food. And the braves cannot shoot only at the English; we will need to hunt the deer soon."

After a small meal of rabbit and berries, Tamoset walked from the swamp island and climbed a nearby knoll. Once at the top, he could look down and see their little camp. He already knew he would advise Philip to abandon this hiding place before the whites found the spot. Yes, Napatoo was right, they must move, but would it be to escape the fighting or start new battles?

Settling himself down on a large flat rock he looked up at the sky. By staring into the heavens, he felt closer to the Creator. Some people, usually leaders or tribal healers, said they had visions or heard words, but Tamoset meditated merely to feel the presence of the Spirit. The one vision he had, he tried to forget, and doubted he would have more.

A summer's breeze whispered through the pines behind him. Tamoset let the wind, sky and earth bring him the peace he so needed. He lay watching as twilight gave way to night, and a sliver of a moon appeared through the haze. The silence washed over him. The good smell of earth and pine soothed him. He gave thanks for the good things in life; the fish, birds, four-legged animals, trees, sun, moon and stars. Hours slipped by, and near midnight, he felt satisfied he could counsel Philip wisely.

* * * *

The next morning, Philip arrived with a small band of warriors. He and Tamoset walked to the far side of the camp where they could not be overheard by the curious. Tamoset noticed Philip seemed more confident than ever. In fact, he could feel Philip's energy and optimism. A necklace of polished shells hung over his breast muscles, and two hawk feathers dangled from the single braid of black hair. At his waist was a metal knife, a new acquisition taken from an Englishman he had killed.

"The English are cowards," sneered Philip, "They stay on the trail, afraid of the forest."

He lit a clay pipe and passed it to Tamoset for the first draw. "They walk into one ambush after another, then leave their wounded and run to get more men."

Contempt spilled from his voice like snake venom. He had always suspected the English would not know how to fight. Now he would make them pay.

Tamoset nodded. A hawk screeched above, soaring. For a moment Tamoset thought about telling Philip of his vision, but then decided on another tack.

"Yes, the white men are easy to kill, especially here in the country we know best. But the whites are like the herring in a springtime river run; for every one we catch, a hundred more still come."

Philip spat on the ground, then boomed, "Let them come! They will meet the same fate as the ones we killed yesterday!"

An awkward silence followed. Philip knew Tamoset was offering the council he had come to rely on. But the time was past for words, for caution, and for second-guessing. Philip looked at his friend, knowing that he too hated the whites.

Tamoset was about to speak, but Philip put his hand up and said, "After all these years we are finally avenging what they have done. The Sickness, the loss of land, the death of my brother."

Tamoset thought of his father, the way he had suffered from the white man's disease. He was not angry at Philip. He had said what needed to be spoken, but Philip had made his decision.

They smoked quietly together as they had done so many times before. Then Tamoset said, "If your mind is made up, then I will fight alongside you. Until the end."

"Not the end," replied Philip, putting his hand on Tamoset's shoulder, "until we drive them out."

Tamoset told him about the villagers: how much food they had, the boys he had posted as guards, and what the elders were saying. He did not tell him of Napatoo's thoughts.

As he looked at Philip he couldn't help thinking that this was his friend's finest hour. He remembered that, even as a boy, Philip talked of one day sending the whites back across the sea, that a great war must someday be fought. Now it had started, and Philip was living out his destiny.

Philip showed not the least doubt that the final outcome would be total annihilation of the whites. His conviction and boldness were contagious, and as their talk continued Tamoset felt ready to take to the warpath. He knew doubts would creep back later, but now he could only marvel at his friend's persuasiveness ... and hope that he was right.

Next, they discussed future actions. Philip used his knife to draw a crude map in the dirt, circling the English town of Rehobeth as the place to strike next. Tamoset agreed, but said the swamp camp must be abandoned, that sooner or later the soldiers would find its location.

"Yes," said Philip, nodding at his friend, "we will leave the swamp and head northwestward to Nipmuck Country. I'll send word to you when to lead them out."

"I think we should send runners ahead to tell the Nipmucks we are coming," suggested Tamoset.

"Haven't you heard?" asked Philip with a broad smile, "The Nipmucks are going to attack the town of Mendon near the headwaters of the Quinobeguin River, the one the English call the Charles. They will welcome us as allies."

Philip's eyes shown with pride. He was as quick to smile as he was to give his icy stare. Today, he was in a fine mood, supremely confident, especially now that another tribe was planning action against the English.

Philip was a warrior if ever there was one. He was the only man Tamoset knew who was genuinely without fear. When other men froze in battle, Philip took needless risks. Those that didn't know him thought he was suicidal, but Tamoset knew he lived for the fight. He had never backed down, and living under the constraints of the English laws had always eaten away at his dignity. Now he was finally fighting back, and he couldn't be happier.

Tamoset turned his gaze from Philip, wondering if his friend could unite the braves in battle. He knew that each brave fought as an individual, and there was little coordination among braves once action began. Philip could whip up the flames of hatred against the English, but could he control them? Each warrior was first loyal to his own sachem. Still, the fact that the Nipmucks were independently attacking the English was a good sign. Hope was in the air.

Chapter 4

Tamoset worked on a white stone, carefully striking it with a larger rock, using quick, powerful flicks of his wrist. The noonday sun made the quartz twinkle and shine, and the flying flakes looked like sparks from a fire. Slowly, with each successive chip, the outline of the arrowhead became clear.

Two other men, both quite old, were working beside him. Lying on the ground between them were two dozen finished stone points and four tomahawk heads.

Tamoset enjoyed the work as well as the conversation of the elders. All felt relieved that they would soon be leaving the swamp camp.

"The braves will have more arrows than they can use," said the older of the two men, his bony arms working swiftly with the stone.

Tamoset chuckled, "So long as their aim is true."

"They won't need great skill; the whites are stupid. They bunch up on the trail. Easy to shoot. Make much noise ... ."

A commotion of voices came from the center of the camp.

"What's that? Is Philip back again?" asked the old man.

Tamoset was already on his feet, running. One of the young boys, stationed as a lookout, had just sprinted into camp.

"I see many soldiers! Just beyond the second stream!" he shouted excitedly.

Tamoset, recognizing that the boy was somewhat hysterical, put his hand on the boy's shoulder and asked, "How many soldiers? Do they run or walk?"

"They walk," said the boy, still gasping for air. "I don't know how many. Muskets, many muskets!"

Tamoset called out for Ponotuck to assist him in organizing a war party to engage the soldiers, but his friend could not be found. He would have to do this on his own. Old men and teenage boys were all he had to work with.

Women began calling for their children, as fear spread through the camp.

"Listen to me!" shouted Tamoset. "I will take twenty men and meet the enemy on the trail. It is better to fight them as far from the camp as possible."

Then, as a way of reassuring the people, he added, "As soon as the English see us, they will scatter. They are expecting women and children, not arrows."

A woman in the crowd cried out, "But what if they do not turn back?"

"They will," barked Tamoset, annoyed. But being ever prudent, he had to plan for the worst. "Hide in the swamp until we return. Be brave; Philip is depending on us."

He led his rag-tag war party sloshing through the swamp, confident that they could circle behind the soldiers and surprise them from the rear. To do so meant trudging through the mud and muck, too shallow to float a canoe.

He pushed the men and boys as fast as they could go. It was imperative to attack the troops before they reached the camp. If the force of English was as large as the young runner said, the whites would probably turn on Tamoset's war party and pursue them in a direction that led away from the women and children.

When Tamoset felt his men were somewhere behind the soldiers, he led them to dry ground, the only trail through the swamp. Mosquitoes were fierce beneath the dark understory of trees, and the air was humid, thick and heavy.

Instructing his men to remain hidden, Tamoset went ahead to reconnoiter.

He didn't have to go far. A hundred yards down the path, he spotted the column of soldiers. It appeared that they had stopped marching and were awaiting orders.

With heart pounding, Tamoset quietly skirted the trail, creeping through the blow-down of tangled trees and brush until he was abreast of the English.

He was relieved to see that they were not a large party at all; he counted only fifteen soldiers who were now gathering around their leader.

Tamoset was no more than twenty-five feet away, and he could clearly see the soldiers were uneasy, each one gripping his musket tightly with both hands.

An older man with white hair was in charge, addressing the group in a low voice, while gesturing up the trail.

Sweat trickled down Tamoset's brow and into his eye, as he slowly notched an arrow in his bow. Rather than lose this opportunity, he decided to act on his own. He hoped his braves, waiting in the rear, would come running when the English fired their muskets.

Telling himself that this was no different from hunting the deer, he pulled back on his bow, letting the arrow fly.

The soldier with the white hair let out a scream that echoed through the forest. Hit directly in the stomach, the man immediately buckled over, landing on his side.

A chill passed over Tamoset as he watched blood spew from the man's wound. He remained frozen in his crouched position and dared not move a muscle. The whites had all raised their muskets, but they didn't know where to shoot—it was as if the arrow had come from the swamp itself.

"Captain, Captain!" cried an Englishman in terror, eyes fixed on his fallen comrade.

But the captain did not stir. Blood trickled from his mouth and continued to gush from his stomach, where only the feathers of the arrow could be seen.

The soldiers formed an outward-facing circle around their stricken captain. One man, however, made no attempt to defend himself, and instead was sobbing loudly as he knelt next to the dying man. This was the captain's son.

Ironically this young man was second in command. When the settlers had formed their militias, leaders were picked for their standing in the community, rather than their knowledge of the forest or experience in battle. Fortunately a tall, thin farmer named John Homer stepped forward and took charge.

"Easy boys, just watch the bushes," he said softly. Homer scanned the trees and bushes, expecting the Indians to come storming out from the foliage at any moment. He logically, but incorrectly, assumed they were about to be ambushed and worried the defensive ring they had formed would make easy targets.

"All right, we're getting out of here," he growled. "Two of you grab the captain—drag him if you have to, but stay with us."

The group slowly turned and fell in behind Homer, muskets ready. No more than fifty feet down the trail they rounded a bend and marched straight into Tamoset's braves, who had heard the captain's scream a minute earlier and were racing to its source.

Even the Indians were somewhat caught off guard by coming face to face with the enemy so suddenly, but they instinctively scattered from the path, taking shelter in the woods.

The blood drained from Homer's face, and a chill went down his spine. Arrows came raining down, one striking the man next to him in the neck, another thumping into the ground an inch from Homer's boot. For a second Homer stood frozen, knowing they were trapped in an ambush, with Indians to the front and rear. Another soldier toppled over, and Homer found his voice; "Fire! For God's sake fire your pieces!"

Without taking aim three men fired wildly into the bushes, while Homer searched for a target.

At that moment, Tamoset came running down the path to help his tribesmen. Out of the corner of his eye, Homer saw him coming, and wheeling around, fired off a shot.

Tamoset stopped in his tracks, lifting his hands to his head. Crimson blood oozed out between his fingers. So soon I go, he thought. He sank to his knees. Napatoo's image flickered before him as darkness closed in.

Some of the Indians saw Tamoset fall, and they let out a blood-curdling cry. They pressed toward the soldiers, sending arrows pouring in like rain. Another Englishman fell with an arrow in his thigh, and while writhing on the ground two more arrows found their mark.

Homer had seen enough. "Stay with me, men! We've got to get past them or we're dead! Show courage!"

This seemed to rally the soldiers, sensing as Homer did that if they didn't move, they would be annihilated. They steadied themselves and opened fire. A fifteen-year-old brave was blown off his feet by a shot that tore open his chest.

Homer grabbed the dead soldier and began to drag him down the path, but dropped him when an arrow whistled by his head and another nicked his arm. Smoke from the muskets obscured his vision and he could see no Indians, but still the arrows came.

One soldier sprinted off the path and into the woods to escape the arrows, but within a second Homer heard him scream. They're everywhere, he thought, got to keep moving.

Now the soldiers were in a full rout, running wildly down the path, some dropping their heavy muskets. Homer ran with them, thinking only to get out of the swamp.

* * * *

Napatoo stroked Tamoset's brow with a wet piece of hide. Tears streamed down her face—she could barely recognize her husband. He lay unconscious before her, his head swollen like a pumpkin from the musket ball striking the side of his face.

A shadow crossed the wigwam opening. The Shaman had arrived. He was an ancient, wizened old man whose eyes where

nothing more than slits. Around his head was an elaborate rat-
tlesnake skin headband holding three turkey feathers, and a
pendant, said to have powers, swung from his neck. His face
was painted completely white, giving him a strange, unearthly
look.

Napatoo rose to her feet and bowed her head. "Shaman,
Powwaw, Medicine Man, we need your help. He still has not
waked up."

The Shaman crouched over Tamoset. "I will speak to the
Creator. I will do what I can."

Napatoo left the wigwam and seated herself just outside the
opening. She tried to concentrate on the Great Creator, but
anger at Philip consumed her. The war has just started, she
thought, and already we suffer.

She could hear the Shaman calling softly on the spirits, his
words turning into song. Minutes passed and his song increased
in tempo. Soon it was accompanied by the rattle of a tortoise
shell. The song became louder and louder. Other villagers
joined Napatoo outside the wigwam.

There was a pause in the song and the Shaman shouted to
the Great Spirit, howling between words. Then all was quiet.
The people knew the Shaman was opening his medicine bag—
no one knew what was inside it. This was followed by loud
breathing noises as the Shaman blew into Tamoset's face.

The crowd parted when the Shaman came out of the wigwam. He stroked Napatoo on the head.

"*Kutchimmoke,* be of good cheer," he whispered. Then he
hobbled off.

Napatoo rushed inside. Tamoset was still unconscious. She stroked the sweat from his forehead and prayed harder than ever. She prayed that his time had not yet come, that he was needed by the tribe, that he was needed by Chusett, that he was needed by her.

Three hours later, Tamoset's eyes fluttered open.

* * * *

It took two days before the swelling in Tamoset's face was down enough to allow partial vision in his left eye. The Indians at the battle were certain he had been hit directly in the head, and attributed his good fortune to intervention by the Great Creator.

Stories of Tamoset's courage and daring raced through the swamp camp. But Tamoset was unaware of his celebrity; pain raged through his skull and even the slightest movement sent shock waves through his head.

On the third day, a fever consumed him. Healing herbs and grasses were placed upon the wound by an old woman and her young apprentice, who together treated all the tribe's illnesses after the Shaman had done his work with the spirits.

By the next morning Tamoset was lucid, but his thoughts were dark, remembering the blood that poured like a spring from the white-haired man he had killed. Mixed with these gloomy ruminations of death were feelings of anger and revenge. Not only had braves been killed under his command, but his own face would be terribly scarred for life. He would never forget the tall, lean Englishman who had wheeled around and fired at him.

That morning an important message arrived from Philip. He wanted the swamp camp abandoned immediately. Tamoset asked Ponotuck, who had returned from his solo hunting trip, to help him organize the evacuation.

Within an hour the villagers were on the move. Still weak from fever and pain, Tamoset found it was all he could do just to keep up with the long line of withdrawing villagers. He tried to hide his weakness from Napatoo, but five minutes into the evacuation she called for two teenage boys to help him, and he did not object.

When Tamoset crossed the part of the trail where the battle had been fought, he saw a sight that would fuel future nightmares. Stuck on top of a long pole was the severed head of the white-haired Englishman. Flies swarmed and crawled about the head, making it appear to move. Tamoset knew without asking that this was the work of the young boys and old men who had fought with him.

As soon as they passed the grisly scene, Tamoset called a halt to the procession. It was best to wait until nightfall before continuing. While they waited he slept, with Chusett by his side. He seemed to gain a measure of peace and strength just by having his son so close.

When they resumed walking, Tamoset no longer needed assistance. Under cover of darkness they made their way back to the bay, and, using make-shift rafts and the few canoes they had hidden, paddled themselves across its northernmost section, landing near Swanzey, where the first shots had been fired days earlier.

Then they trudged northwest, to meet Philip and his warriors at a prearranged location. Together they would trek inland to Nipmuck country. The war would be carried to the western frontier.

Chapter 5

The corn was knee high, the peas ripe, and beans were flowering when John Homer returned home to his farm in Medfield. A gentle breeze carried the rich smell of earth on this clear Sunday morning in July.

Homer and five other volunteers in the militia had been walking for a day and half since leaving Swanzey. Despite his exhaustion and the blisters on his feet, he felt his spirits soar now that he could see his fields.

Walking up the path to his home, he thought it odd that none of his six children was playing about. He lifted the wooden latch, opened the house door and hollered, but only his voice echoed back. A sense of dread swept over him. Where were they, he wondered? Surely the Indians hadn't attacked here. Then he smiled with relief; of course, it's the Sabbath, they're at church. Elizabeth, his wife, never missed a service, and he knew she would be fervently praying for his safe return.

Homer decided he, too, would say a prayer of thanks for surviving the swamp skirmish. He knew he was lucky to be alive—had the party of Indians been larger, all the soldiers would have been killed in the ambush. He thought about the short, muscular Indian he shot in the face, and wondered if God really did consider savages sub-human. He remembered his minister comparing the redskins to the devil, saying, "We must follow the righteous ways of the Lord and drive out these painted savages."

Homer wasn't so sure about this philosophy, but he didn't dare speak his thoughts—to do so would mean persecution by the church, colony and the entire village. Better to put these doubts out of mind and enjoy the comfort of being home.

Stuffing his long clay pipe, he strolled over to a large apple tree at the rear of the house and sat down, leaning his back against the trunk. His home was built on a small ridge, and below him, to the west, he could see the the slow brown waters of the River Charles, while to the south was the gentle outline of Noon Hill. Between his home and the hill were acres and acres of fertile wetlands where ducks winged their way over green marsh grass.

The warm morning sun made him drowsy and he lay his pipe down, closed his eyes, thinking of all the wonderful times he and his oldest son, Jeramiah, had hunting and fishing along the river. I'll have to spend a day with the boy, he thought. We haven't been together much lately. He started to drift off to sleep but suddenly opened his eyes and sat upright, rigid against the tree trunk. "Damn," he whispered. A picture of the Indian's bloody face had flashed through his mind, jarring his peacefulness, just as it had done the last three nights.

* * * *

Far to the southwest, the band of Wampanoags moved as rapidly as possible with women, children and a few remaining possessions. At the head of the group were Philip, Tamoset, Napatoo with baby Chusett, and Weetamoo, the matriarch sachem of another band of Wampanoags. Behind them, walking quickly in single file, were at least 150 fellow villagers. They were making haste to reach the Nipmucks to the west, near the English town of Brookfield.

Ponotuck ran up to the front of the line and fell in step with the leaders.

"Where have you been this time?" asked Napatoo sarcastically.

"Someone has to bring in fresh meat," answered Ponotuck with a smile.

Philip turned around. "What meat?"

"I gave some of the women behind us a nice fat sheep," boasted Ponotuck. "I took it from a settler's farm, it was easier than hunting deer. Tonight, we will feast."

Weetamoo shook her head, "There will be no feasting tonight, we must move like the wolf."

"Weetamoo is right," said Philip, "only a short rest tonight and no fires. We will walk with the moon."

They walked on in silence and Philip found himself next to Napatoo. She had Chusett strapped in the pack on her back, and the child was wide-eyed, enjoying the motion and the many shapes and colors that passed in and out of sight.

"Napatoo," said Philip quietly, "you never talk to me anymore."

Napatoo kept walking, eyes straight ahead.

When she didn't answer he whispered, "There was once a time when you loved me."

Her eyes darted about trying to locate Tamoset, but he was at the front of the column, talking with Ponotuck. Her face grew red from anger. How dare he bring that up now, she thought. She waited a few seconds, controlling her anger, then looked directly at him. "The past is gone; I am happy in my marriage to Tamoset."

Her voice was low. "He is the kindest man I ever met, and his love for Chusett knows no bounds."

She paused, eyes back on the trail, then added, "You have your own wife and son."

A small stream had to be crossed and Philip took Napatoo's arm in his to help her over.

She pretended the gesture meant nothing. I should tell him what I think, she thought. It may be the last chance I get. She knew she had to choose her words carefully and decided to begin by talking about her husband, his friend. She kept her voice low, barely above a whisper.

"Tamoset has his doubts about your strategy, but he would never tell you so himself. Have you given him the chance to talk openly? He harbors no ambitions. He does not want to lead the braves."

"We need him," Philip said gruffly.

"I need him, too. You know this war is madness. You didn't even consult the Shaman. What will we eat? What fields will we plant? Will we always be running?"

Philip was in no mood to argue. Napatoo was one of only a few people that could give a differing opinion without being exposed to his rage. Years had passed since their brief and stormy relationship, but she still had a special hold on him.

On the trail ahead, Tamoset glanced back at his wife and decided to join her, sensing something was wrong. He assumed she had probably spoken her mind to Philip, never suspecting there was more to the conversation than a discussion of war.

Philip raised his voice for the group to hear, "Napatoo was just asking me where we will get our food. It's easy—after we attack a farm and kill the whites, we take their food! Look at how Ponotuck got the sheep. Soon it will be the whites who are running from their homes."

"Yes!" echoed Ponotuck, still streaked with red and black warpaint, "We will show the whites our gods are more powerful than theirs. Soon many scalps will be taken along the Great River."

Weetamoo was quietly listening and decided now was the time to tell Philip her plan. She waited for him to come up the trail, and then fell in beside him.

"Philip," she began, "You and Ponotuck are right, you must carry the battle to the long tidal river, the Connecticut. But our old and infirm cannot make such a rigorous journey. I want to take a small band of warriors and lead our women, children and elders to a safer place. I know that Canonchet and the Narragansetts will welcome us."

Philip had not considered this, but immediately saw the wisdom of moving ahead with only those who could travel quickly. Yes, he thought, Canonchet can not refuse women and children. He nodded, placing his hand on her shoulder. "It is a good plan," he said solemnly, "we will split after we rest."

Ponotuck heard the decision and with wide eyes asked, "What are our battle plans, Philip?"

"We will hit them where they are weak, avoiding the large towns. After we hit, we will run, they will follow, and we will be waiting in ambush."

"What towns will we attack?" pressed Ponotuck.

"You ask too many questions. Just worry about how you will perform against whites armed with muskets."

"Don't worry about me," said Ponotuck quickly, breaking into his easy smile. "I will get my share of scalps, maybe a captive, too. I always wanted—what's that? Shots!"

Tamoset ran to the back of the column while Philip led the women and children at full run. Upon reaching the rear, Tamoset could not believe his eyes—Mohegans! They had attacked the end of the Wampanoag procession, killing two braves.

He was about to organize a counterattack, but already the Mohegans were falling back, content with their surprise raid and the plunder dropped by fleeing Wampanoags.

How had they found us, he wondered? They had selected little-known trails for their escape from the Pocasset Swamp, and they had been certain no one knew their whereabouts.

After organizing a rear guard, Tamoset sprinted back to the head of the column and told Philip what he had seen.

"The Mohegans are allies to the English," said a stunned Philip while still running, "How did those cowards know we were here?"

Tamoset shook his head. "They have retreated. I don't think they will attack again. I put some of our best braves at the rear to be on the lookout."

"Good. Keep moving."

* * * *

They camped under some tall pines that night, with scouts stationed every thirty feet along the perimeter. No cooking fires were allowed, and braves kept their weapons close at hand.

Tamoset told Napatoo he needed to discuss something with her, and they asked a friend to look after Chusett. The couple walked beyond earshot of the villagers and sat down on a large granite boulder not far from the perimeter scouts. Crickets chirped loudly in the still summer air, and somewhere in the distance a fox gave its eerie bark.

Tamoset came right to the point. "I want you to take Chusett and follow Weetamoo to the Narragansett camp. You will be safe there."

"But where will you go? We must not separate."

"I'll follow Philip, but I promise to come for you as soon as I can."

Napatoo looked down, shaking her head. "This is a mistake. I should come with you, or we should all go to the Narragansetts. If we stay together we have a chance."

He hated to argue, hated the thought of leaving her. But he was certain his decision was the correct one. "No, I've got to fight with the warriors, there is no choice. It's not safe for you to come with us. You will be out of danger with the Narragansetts. Think of Chusett."

Napatoo took both of his hands, her small face tired from the strain, "I am thinking of Chusett, and I'm thinking of you. You must talk to Philip, we cannot hope to win this war. Look at yourself—your face is terribly scarred, the next musket ball may kill you."

"We have talked of this many times. It's too late for peace."

Napatoo knew it was hopeless. "When will I see you again?"

Tamoset didn't answer, but stared out into the trees. A cloud passed over the moon, shrouding them in total darkness. No sense making any promises, he thought; the future's a mystery. Only the Great Spirit knows what the winds of change will bring. He was about to explain that Philip needed time to organize the tribes, but decided it best not to mention his friend.

They sat on the rock, holding hands silently for many minutes before returning to the others.

Chapter 6

Muttawmp waited at the edge of the Nipmuck village. His small, wide-set eyes scanned the edge of the fields for signs of the Wampanoags. He was still groggy from the night's victory celebration, but felt he must be there to greet Philip. Only an hour earlier a runner had awakened the village to report that Philip was only five miles away. Word had spread like wildfire; the man who had started this war would soon arrive.

Muttawmp was the leader of the Nipmucks—"Fresh Water People"—who lived in this wild area not yet heavily settled by whites. Yesterday had been a great day for his people. First, they had ambushed a party of soldiers, and then they had burned Brookfield to the ground while the inhabitants huddled inside a garrison.

Just as he was about to head back to his wigwam, something caught his eye at the southern end of the cornfield. The Wampanoags were coming! A long line of Indians came out of the forest, led by a tall man he guessed was Philip. They walked slowly, and even at this distance Muttawmp could tell they were exhausted. There was no spring in their step, but Philip walked erect with his head up. By his side was a shorter man with a terrible scar running across one side of his face.

Shouts of "Philip, Philip!" spread from wigwam to wigwam, and soon the entire village gathered behind Muttawmp. They were curious to see the famous Wampanoag leader, and they also wondered how Muttawmp would act. Both men hated the English, but could they share their power, or would one have to lead?

When Philip was within thirty feet, Muttawmp shouted, "So you are Philip, we have heard of your fight!"

"And I have just learned of yours," said Philip, walking closer.

Muttawmp smiled, "Yes, soldiers came looking for us. We found them first."

The crowd let up a mighty cheer. Euphoria was in the air. When the roar died down, Philip looked out at all those gathered and spoke loudly, "We come to fight side by side with our Nipmuck brothers."

Again those assembled voiced their approval, jumping and raising fists to the sky. Philip was everything they heard he was.

Philip gestured to his own tribesmen.

"My people have waited many years for this day. No longer will we beg for scraps from the white man's table. We are tired of being treated like dogs. We will not be cheated and imprisoned any longer. We will not put our mark on the white man's paper—the words on the paper change with time. No, now it's time to pay the English back with blood: their blood!"

The howl that followed slowly turned into a chant of "war, war, war!"

Muttawmp looked beyond Philip at the haggard band of Wampanoags. Raising his voice above the crowd he shouted, "You are welcome here. Word of your bravery at Montaup traveled quickly through the forest. Many tribes gained courage from you. We have sent runners westward to spread the word. Soon all tribes will take to the warpath. Smoke from burning farms will cover the sun."

The Nipmucks went into a spontaneous dance, raising dust into the morning air. Philip glanced at Tamoset as if to say, "See, other tribes are joining us."

Muttawmp gestured to Philip, and together they walked toward the sachem's wigwam.

"Our village is open to you," said Muttawmp. "You and your people must rest. We have much food from our celebration. Eat, rest and refresh yourselves. Tonight we will meet and decide where to strike next."

Chapter 7

While Nipmuck women worked quickly to serve their guests, adding more food to the cooking pots, the Wampanoags lay their few possessions down at the end of the village, relieved to be so warmly welcomed. The sun was quite strong, and Tamoset sprawled on the ground, resting after the long journey.

He felt like years had passed since the war started, as if the simpler days of just a few weeks earlier had happened in a different life. Other braves were intoxicated by all the recent action, but the excitement came in small snatches for him, sandwiched between hours of contemplation and concern. He wondered about the upcoming council between Philip and Muttawmp, guessing that a decision would be made to travel farther west, farther from Napatoo.

The Nipmuck women arrived with the stew, but even while eating, Tamoset's mind was on Napatoo. I'm changing already, he thought. I haven't smiled in days. He felt like a bear in autumn, all business before hibernation. Napatoo. Did she make it to the Narragansetts? Does she know I'm safe? Somehow, he thought, I've got to get word to her.

After devouring the venison stew, flavored with wild onions and turnips, the exhausted Wampanoags drifted off to sleep. But Tamoset, feeling on edge, knew that sleep would elude him, so he decided to see more of the village.

He walked down the main path, passing row after row of wigwams. The Wampanoags were not the only tired ones; the Nipmucks were resting after the all-night celebration. Except for the guards posted around the outskirts of the village, most people were asleep. Even the dogs were quiet. Some warriors rested in the sunshine, while others dozed in their wigwams.

It was a fine August afternoon, with clear blue skies; the kind of day Tamoset usually spent hunting. The country of the Nipmuck had subtle differences than his own. There were more hills and denser forests. The streams were swifter, clearer. He liked this land. In a better time it would be good to explore.

Far up ahead he could see the edge of the corn and bean fields. He had always been interested in agriculture and his fellow villagers often sought his advice when a particular crop was not doing well. Tamoset was unusual in that he often helped Napatoo in their garden. The men in the village wondered why he would concern himself with something that was women's work. Although they joked and teased him, they did so with a smile—Tamoset was slow to anger but they didn't want to test him. Besides his strength, it was also known that he was Philip's closest friend and confidant.

When he reached the edge of the field he smiled with satisfaction. The Nipmucks had chosen a fertile meadow next to a river where the corn was in its prime. Golden tassels waved gently in the breeze, and the dark green leaves made a soft rustling sound. Just being near these growing things lifted his spirits.

In the middle of the field was a platform, roughly five feet high, with a small roof of reeds to provide shade from the summer sun. Children's voices and laughter could be heard coming from the inside. He could see their heads through the large side openings and decided to wander over.

The structure was built to serve as a lookout to spot marauding crows, woodchucks and rabbits. Children were assigned shifts in the platform where they were supposed to keep a constant vigil over the precious crops.

As effective as the structures were as lookout stations, the children thought of them as their own private huts where they played forbidden games and told jokes their parents said were bad. It was obvious to Tamoset that that's what the children were doing just now. Whispers were followed by uncontrolled giggles.

The children, too absorbed in their stories, did not notice Tamoset approaching. He threw a pebble on the roof so they wouldn't be too surprised. Four little heads immediately turned and looked his way.

They didn't say a word. Who was this stranger with a purple-red scar?

"Let me borrow your bow and arrow," said Tamoset softly.

The children were frightened now, but the oldest girl grabbed the bow and tossed it to him, then did the same with an arrow.

When Tamoset notched the arrow on the bow string, two of the children ducked down, while the others watched with trepidation as the stranger walked to the front of the platform and then pulled back on the bow, letting the arrow fly.

The arrow whizzed 70 feet toward a small mound of dirt. The woodchuck never knew what hit him.

Scrambling off the platform, the children raced to the struggling rodent. The older girl had a baby in a pack on her back.

A boy of nine or ten reached the animal first, picked up a large stone, and put an end to the woodchuck's writhing.

The boy was beaming. He picked the animal up and presented it to Tamoset.

"No, not mine," said Tamoset with a grin, "the one who kills it keeps it."

A wide, toothy smile spread across the boy's face—he could already hear his father's praise.

Now the children were talking all at once.

"How did you see the groundhog?"

"We thought you were going to shoot us!"

The youngest boy was staring at Tamoset, "What happened to your face?" he asked bluntly.

The older girl slapped the boy on the side of the head. "Don't be so bold," she admonished.

Tamoset's hand ran along his scar line; he had forgotten how he looked. He looked down at the young boy and smiled. "It's a fair question. This is what happens when somebody shoots at you. Woodchucks are not the only ones who have enemies."

The boy who killed the woodchuck was sitting on the ground, trying to get the arrow out of the animal without breaking it. He looked up at Tamoset, shielding his eyes from the sun. "It was the English who did that, wasn't it?"

Tamoset nodded.

The arrow came free and the boy held it up, declaring, "I want to kill an Englishman."

Tamoset decided to change the subject. Looking at the girl, he said, "Let me see the baby."

The girl turned sideways, showing the wide head of a baby boy, sleeping soundly.

For a moment Tamoset couldn't speak. The emotion of seeing the baby, who looked so much like Chusett, overwhelmed him. He stroked the child's fuzzy black hair, then ran his fingertips down his soft, fat cheeks.

Tamoset looked back at the children. He knew they had no idea of the trouble that would soon be coming. His eyes were moist and he started walking off, turning back to say, "You are good children, take care of each other."

His sudden departure caught them by surprise, and they looked at each other quizzically. This Wampanoag was very different, they thought.

Chapter 8

Bean plants spiraled up many of the cornstalks—a novel growing idea—but Tamoset didn't notice. He quietly walked toward
the back of the field. Seeing the baby with the Nipmuck children made him yearn for his own boy, to hold him in his arms
where he would always be safe.

He felt unstable, adrift—feelings he had never known before. His inherent confidence seemed to abandon him, replaced
by doubts. Somewhere deep inside a voice was nagging, "Get
out, Tamoset, go back to Montaup."

Far off in the distance, he could hear a chopping noise
coming from the river. He turned and headed toward it.

Approaching the river, he first saw the long white hair of an
old man who was hunched over a log, rhythmically swinging a
curved stone axe. Tamoset greeted the man.

The old man glanced up and grunted his acknowledgement,
never missing a swing.

A fire pit, filled with red, glowing embers, smouldered next
to the large pine log that was to become a canoe. After a few
more chops, the old man placed his axe aside. He fanned the
coals, and then, using a wooden shovel, transferred a scoopful
of embers onto the log. The slow burn of the coals would help
hollow the inside of the canoe.

The old man looked at Tamoset. "Sit on the back of the log, I need you to steady it."

Tamoset did as he was told, noticing the deep lines in the face of the Nipmuck. Years of exposure to both weather and wood smoke made his skin look like old leather.

"I am Ochala. Who are you?"

"Tamoset. I'm a Wampanoag."

Ochala picked up the axe and began rounding the front of the log. Every muscle in his forearm could be seen, and Tamoset marveled at the little man's strength. Each short chop sent a wood chip flying. The same chips would later be gathered and fed to the coals so that the log was actually helping to transform itself into a canoe.

"Drop some chips on the coals," instructed Ochala between chops.

Tamoset reached sideways, and for the first time Ochala noticed the scar. The fresh look of the wound caused the old man to assume that it was the work of the English. He stopped hacking and suddenly said, "We are no match for the English."

Tamoset wasn't sure what the crusty old man said and cocked his head quizzically.

Ochala looked Tamoset in the eye, "You were injured by the English?"

"Yes."

"We will lose this war."

Tamoset was startled by his abruptness. "Why so certain?" he asked.

"Because we will be fighting both the English and other tribes. Do you think the Mohawks will join us? Never. They will use this as an opportunity to gain favor from the English. Even some of our own tribesmen will turn against us."

Tamoset had wondered about the same thing.

Ochala fanned the embers, and he scooped another shovelful into the log. "The Nipmucks and Wampanoags are but a few against many enemies. I remember the Pequots fought the English long ago—today there are farms where they once lived."

"Then you are against the war?" asked Tamoset.

"No. We have to try. To do nothing is worse."

They worked in silence for a time. Ochala looked up at the sun, "Enough for today. I think I will be coming back to hide the canoe. It is probable that Muttawmp will take us west. You and I will talk again."

The old man headed toward the village, and Tamoset walked the opposite way on the riverside path. He reflected on Ochala's gloomy predictions, but nature's wonders were also calling for his attention. The river was one of the most beautiful he had ever seen. It tumbled over boulders creating small falls and pools, making gurgling sounds pleasing to his ear. The water glistened and sparkled where the sun broke through the canopy of foliage above.

Tamoset's mood brightened with each passing step—so much life to be seen, signs that the Great Creator favored this land. A kingfisher winged its way down the river, and a heron stood motionless on the opposite shore. Tamoset saw it all. He knew the sacred creatures—bear, cougar and eagle—were also nearby. His eyes read the story: a scattering of feathers where the cougar had killed a partridge; bear tracks in the sand; and the skull of a fish picked clean by an eagle, a feather by its side.

When he rounded the next bend, he suddenly stopped. Up ahead lay a large pool bathed in sunlight, with a woman standing at the water's edge. First, she removed her moccasins, and then her doe-skin dress. Tamoset stared wide-eyed at her well-toned legs and buttocks. Straight black hair flowed half way down her back. As she turned to face the water, he saw her large, firm breasts.

She walked to a large boulder and effortlessly leaped to its flat top. Her movements were graceful, cat-like and surprisingly quick. She looked upward for a second, perhaps in silent prayer, and then dove.

Tamoset stood mesmerized. But when she failed to surface, he stepped forward in alarm. He scanned the rippling water; was she hurt? More seconds went by, and he wondered if he had imagined the whole thing, a dream, or a vision perhaps?

She broke the water just ten feet in front of him, catching him by surprise. She stood in chest deep water, looking directly at him.

"Who are you," she demanded in a deep, clear voice.

"I, I was … ."

She didn't let him finish. "What are you doing here?"

"When you did not come up, I grew concerned."

"So," she said accusingly, "You have been watching me the whole time."

Tamoset hesitated, then stammered, "I'm a Wampanoag, I … ."

"This is the area where women bathe. You should have asked before wandering around our village."

Tamoset could see she was both embarrassed and angry, and getting madder by the minute. He thought it best to leave and turned back on the path.

Upon reaching the spot where Ochala's half-finished canoe lay, he stopped and sat by the river. As attractive as this country was, he would never feel at home in the land of the Nipmucks. His afternoon had not gone well. Only the children had made him feel comfortable, and even that was a bittersweet meeting, seeing the baby so much like Chusett. Ochala's greeting had been one of pessimism. The old man had said, "We will talk again." But of what, more doleful predictions?

And then there was the girl. Never had he seen a woman like her. Physically, she seemed to combine strength with grace, and even in her anger, he could see the beauty and intelligence in her eyes. Seeing her only made him miss Napatoo more. Yet at the same time he was attracted to the girl—any man would be. The thought troubled him, and he tried to push it from his mind.

As if to emphasize his confusion, a dark cloud passed in front of the sun. Tamoset looked upward, not a rain cloud but an enormous flock of birds. Passenger pigeons. Truly an unbelievable sight—more than a million birds. Now they were directly above and so many wings sounded like thunder. He lay back and watched. The flock kept coming, minute after minute, then suddenly it passed and the sun was back. "Perhaps," he told himself, "my problems, too, are just passing shadows."

* * * *

Minutes later he heard a twig snap somewhere behind him, and he wheeled around.

It was Ponotuck, running. "Tamoset!" he shouted out of breath, "I've been looking all over for you. Philip wants to talk with you. He and Muttawmp have decided we must go west to the Great River."

"When?" asked Tamoset, thinking how he was getting further and further from Napatoo.

"Tomorrow. They say the Pocumtucks, Norwottucks and Squakheags will join us there."

Tamoset stood, and the two men ran back to the village. He guessed Philip would want to have him help lead the trek westward. There would be no discussion about whether the decision was right or wrong. He knew that once Philip made up his mind the topic was closed. That was one reason why he was so effective: those around him could feel his confidence, feel his conviction, and it was easy to follow.

"I almost forgot," Ponotuck said turning toward Tamoset as they ran, "Napatoo and the others are safe, they have been accepted by Canonchet and now live with the Narragansetts."

Tamoset broke into a wide grin, "It is a good day, my friend. A good day after all."

Chapter 9

Now that the natives' rage was uncorked, John Homer doubted anything could stop it from spreading. He had little hope that the rebellion could be put down quickly; in fact, from all reports it appeared the natives were winning. This did not surprise him—the soldiers were fighting in the traditional European style, and they were slow to adjust to the hit-and-run tactics of the natives.

But at this moment his attention was focused on a large pine stump which sat in the middle of a lush green meadow he was clearing. The stump had been too large to drag out of the ground even with the aid of his horse, so he decided to burn it. But before he could put it to the torch, he and his son Jeramiah first had to clear the dirt away from its sides so the fire could breathe.

It was backbreaking work, and an unusually hot autumn day made it all the harder. But this was the last of the stumps to be burned from the field by the banks of the Charles. First they had felled the virgin timber, dragging it by horse to a nearby sawmill for cutting into planks. Then the smaller stumps were cleared, and the larger ones were burned.

The final task would be to remove the many rocks that littered the bony soil, and form them into a wall to mark the property and fence in sheep and cattle. In spite of the miles of stone walls, livestock was constantly getting loose, and the town pounds were always full. Neighboring natives had long complained that the settlers' cattle were trampling their fields of corn and vegetables, but little had been done.

Someday, Homer hoped to build a larger barn and raise more cattle. His 150-acre farm had only twenty cleared acres, but the rich marsh grass growing by the wetlands was excellent cattle feed. And at the north end of his land, he had begun to dig a series of small ditches to drain more marsh for pastureland. The small alders and willows that grew there could be easily burned. He also considered building a small mill on a stream which ran through the center of his land. But these dreams of progress would have to wait—first the war with the natives must be won.

"Is it true father, about Brookfield?" asked Jeremiah between hoisting shovelfuls of dirt.

"I'm afraid so. The town lays in ashes, and only by the grace of God did any villagers survive."

"What will happen next?"

" 'Tis more trouble to be sure, son. I've heard there've been attacks in the Connecticut River Valley."

Jeremiah stopped shoveling. A worried look spread over his young face. "Will you be going off with the militia again?"

Homer ceased digging and motioned for the boy to sit down with him on a nearby boulder. "Don't worry. I'm not going out west. I may be needed here, though. Things have been quiet, but I fear there's trouble brewin'. It's best I stay close to home."

"Christopher Harkin told me in Natick they're rounding up all the Praying Indians and carting them off to prison."

"It's true. That's what I meant by trouble being stirred up. We have enough trouble with Philip's Indians—now they go and imprison the friendly ones. Word will reach the other neutral Indians and they will be forced to choose sides. We both know what they will do."

Natick lay just a few river miles downstream. It was the site of one of the largest "Praying Indian" communities, where natives who had converted to Christianity were being taught to live like whites. While progress had been slow, the settlement was prospering—until the war started. Panic-stricken settlers demanded that the peaceful natives of Natick be arrested and imprisoned. Hate ruled the day, and the natives were rounded up and incarcerated on an island in Boston Harbor.

Father and son went back to work, both thinking about the days to come. The events in Natick reminded them that though the war was now being fought out west, incidents were happening nearby that would have repercussions. Homer was angered by most of the policies coming out of Boston, but he knew the importance of killing Philip quickly. His farm could be threatened, possibly his family, and he wanted things to go back to the way they were. He would do whatever was needed to protect the life he had carved out of the wilderness.

* * * *

That evening Homer went to the town's tavern to hear the latest news. Inside, a fat man from Boston was talking quite loudly. He had been trading information from the outside world for free ale, paid for by the small group of locals who listened to his every word.

"I tell you they had at least fifty Indians right there in the middle of Boston Common. Mostly squaws and children. We should have shot them on the spot, but those devils shall get better than they deserve. 'Tis said they will be sold as slaves and shipped to the West Indies."

The boisterous Bostonian paused to sip his beer. Beads of persperation clung to his forehead. It wasn't everyday that he held center stage, and with each mug of ale he enjoyed it more. Filled with his new found self-importance, he continued: "The squaws wore only doeskin skirts and were naked from the middle up. I must admit, some of the heathens weren't half bad-looking. They looked stupid though, staring off into the distance."

"Aye, perhaps they thought their braves would stroll into Boston and save them!" one of the locals said sarcastically. A ripple of snickers and guffaws rose from the group.

"I don't think so," bellowed the Bostonian quickly. "Some of their braves were there—except they forgot their bodies. Their heads were stuck on poles!"

The men pounded wooden tankards and roared with laughter, except for Homer who stood off to one side. He was about to leave when one of the Medfield men said he saw a native skulking about on nearby Noon Hill.

"And when did you see this Indian?" asked Homer.

All heads turned toward him. The group had not noticed him standing at the rear of the dimly lit tavern, and they now nodded a polite greeting. They had considered Homer a simple farmer until they heard of his actions in the fight with the Wampanoags near Swanzey.

The Medfield man elaborated on his Indian sighting: "It was just two days ago. I raised my musket to kill the swine, but the coward slipped off into the brush before I could get a shot. Narragansett, I think it was."

"Those bastard Narragansetts aren't to be trusted," barked the Bostonian, feeling compelled to stand up in an effort to regain his audience. "I hear that they're using this opportunity to steal from isolated farms. But we can't get back at them because that damn Roger Williams and his blasphemous Quakers don't want trouble. Williams has been appeasing those bloody red devils for too long! Sooner or later we're going to have to do God's work and rid them from our land."

Homer felt compelled to speak, "Well, that may be, but we best secure Medfield first. I'd guess the Wampanoags and Nipmucks might be coming east again and we ought be ready."

For the first time the tavern owner spoke up, "He's right, we should get the garrison ready and have the cannon primed. It wouldn't surprise me if the whole Connecticut River Valley goes up in smoke. We best be prepared. Our soldiers should have listened to that Ben Church fellow from Plymouth and ended the war at Swanzey. Instead, we let Philip escape, and now he's got Nipmucks, Norrowatucks and just about every other Injun tribe on his side."

The Bostonian changed the subject, telling of the recent penalties handed out to the Quakers. "A repeat offender got a hole bored through his tongue with a red hot iron and his wife got thirty lashes. That ought to keep them out of the colony!"

Homer had heard it all before. He raised the door latch and slipped out as the group once again laughed and enjoyed their ale.

The night air had cooled considerably. Homer loved this time of year; the harvest, the vivid foliage, and the fine hunting for deer and a wide assortment of ducks that were migrating southward. He took a deep breath of the pungent, musky air, glad to be away from the Bostonian. He had hoped for quiet conversation with his friend, the tavern owner, not a speech on war from a man who probably didn't even own a musket.

It was only a mile walk back to farm, but the talk of natives in the area caused him to be more alert than usual. A full moon shone down, lighting his way on the dirt road. An owl hooted from a nearby pine, and Homer quickened his step. He thought of the ambush at the swamp, and a chill went through him, remembering his comrades screaming as arrows brought them down.

When he reached his farm he rapped on the door. His wife, Elizabeth, asked who it was before she pulled back the bolt and raised the oak cross latch. Wrapping her arms around him, she whispered, "I worry so when you are out. This war makes me afraid, I pray for its end every day."

She had been sewing by the light of a small fire and a lone candle. The six children were all in bed. For the first time, she was afraid to be alone on the farm.

Helping him with his coat, she asked, "What news have you?"

Homer pulled a chair up next to Elizabeth's and they sat by the fire. "I listened to some fat pig from Boston act like he was winning the war single-handedly. Chances are, he's never seen an Indian warrior in his life. He talked of the Indian captives that were brought to Boston to be shipped to the Indies, but he really didn't have any news from Springfield. I sometimes get the feeling that the colony is relieved to have the fighting be out west, and isn't doing much to help those poor souls."

"John, you're not thinking of joining the militia that's heading out there, are you?"

"No. Not now anyway. But I sense we are going to loose this war unless we change our tactics. We need to fight like Indians to beat Indians."

"Lord knows, all I want is peace. I don't even care about winning. Can't we just go back to the way things were?"

"I'm afraid not. 'Tis a war to the finish, I fear. The Colony will never forgive the Indians. And the Indians have tasted victory. I'm sure they believe they can drive us out. Think of their bitterness from being cheated out of everything from beaver pelts to land."

"But did they have to start this bloodshed? And their torture is worse than the devil itself could do."

"Are we any better? We have our own set of cruelties—and we do it to each other in the name of religion," said Homer with a sigh, thinking of the Quakers.

Elizabeth was clearly uncomfortable with such talk. It was dangerous to question the laws of the colony. She worried one of the children might be listening up in the loft. "Let's get to bed, you've had a long day."

Homer nodded, "I'll be there in a minute."

But he wasn't. He lit his pipe and sat staring into the fire.

Chapter 10

From the top of what the English called Sugarloaf Mountain, Tamoset could see a broad vista southward along the Connecticut River. Like a ribbon of blue, the river snaked through the rich, flat bottomland below. He watched whiffs of smoke drift upward from three tiny clearings where settlers had built their homesteads. The smoke was not from cooking fires, but from the smouldering ruins of the cabins which the natives had burned during the past two days.

Warriors had been streaming into Philip's and Muttawmp's new river camp from all directions. Using it as a base of operations, small groups of braves fanned out into the surrounding countryside to attack nearby farms. A dozen scalps were hanging in the riverside camp.

Tamoset was with five Nipmuck warriors deciding where they would raid. Deerfield had already been hit, and the remaining whites were staying close to the garrison house. But at some of the isolated farms to the southeast, the families were not aware that so large a number of natives was amassed nearby. For years these farmers had lived in peace with their native neighbors, so they tended to believe that the troubles they had heard about in Brookfield and Swanzey would not happen here.

The small band of warriors decided to cross the river and travel a few miles southeastward, attacking the first farm they came to. It was now early September, and the leaves of the swamp maples showed a touch of crimson. Tamoset reflected that in normal years this should be a happy time for his people: crops were harvested and safely stored, hunting was excellent, and the village had time for festivities. How odd it was to be roaming the woods with five men from a strange tribe, looking for whites to kill.

Yet he was excited about this offensive action and anxious to take revenge on the people who had caused him to flee his home. Since he had left Montaup, his own life had meant little—he was now living to protect his wife and child. He reasoned that every white man he could kill would give his son a better chance when it was his turn to face the invaders.

Dressed only in breech clouts, and carrying nothing but tomahawks, bows and arrows, the Indians swallowed up the miles as late afternoon turned to evening. With dusk came the heavy, dank scents of the earth and vegetation, and the group moved ghost-like through the forest.

The tall Nipmuck leading the band, called Poxset, suddenly stopped trotting and raised his hand for the others to do the same. A faint scent of wood smoke was detected in the autumn air. They crept forward cautiously. Up ahead was a small, stump-filled clearing. At the far end of the field stood a box-like log cabin. Yellow light filtered through two windows, no more than a foot wide.

Inside the home a woman was busy getting her children to bed. "Put your blocks away, Sybil," said the mother to her young daughter. "Noah, leave the dog alone and climb into bed."

Three-year-old Noah gave his mother a sly look and pulled the dog's tail one more time before shuffling toward the mattress stuffed with dried grass and hay.

When the children had settled down, the woman tucked them in and then opened her Bible to begin the nightly reading. At the other side of the room her husband was busy by the light of the fire, scraping down a fox skin.

Suddenly the dog growled, and the entire family looked up at once. The growl turned into a bark, and the man jumped for his musket above the fireplace. As he filled it with powder and shot, his wife pleaded, "Ezekial, don't you dare go out there!"

"I've got no choice. It could be a wolf or cougar after our cow. I'm not going to stand by and let our only cow be killed."

"A cow doesn't matter, its not ... ."

He stopped her in midsentence with a stern look and slowly lifted the latch. He opened the door and stood for a second, staring into the darkness. The dog growled behind him.

Suddenly he gasped sharply in pain, and staggered backward, three arrows sticking from his chest. His wife screamed in terror, while the children, too stunned to even cry, watched the blood pour from their father. The woman rushed for the door, but the Indians were already piling through, knocking her to the floor.

The dog's snarls were cut short by a tomahawk blow to the head by Poxset, the first Indian to enter. Poxset waved his tomahawk, and turned on the children. Sybil and Noah shrieked at the sight of the huge Nipmuck, and their mother scrambled up, instinctively throwing herself on them. The Nipmuck leader leaped after her and split her head with a vicious swing, spilling her brains upon the children.

Lying on the floor, the farmer tried to raise himself but was instantly killed when Tamoset buried his tomahawk deep in the man's skull.

The Nipmucks were ransacking the cabin, and Tamoset turned his attention to the children who were clinging to each other in horror. He grabbed both children to take them captive, but Poxset would have none of it.

"Down!" barked the Nipmuck leader, motioning for Tamoset to drop the children. Tamoset wheeled around to face him but the Nipmuck acted first, clubbing the boy then the girl. Stunned, Tamoset released his grip on the bodies and they fell to the floor with a thud.

Angered by this act of cruelty, Tamoset took a step toward Poxset. Immediately all five Nipmucks raised their tomahawks, smiling, waiting to see what Tamoset would do.

"Leave now if you want to live," hissed Poxset through clinched teeth. Tamoset wavered for a moment, but then backed toward the door. He knew they were seconds away from hacking him to pieces.

When he reached the edge of the field, he looked back at the house and saw that the Nipmucks had set it ablaze. Sparks were already shooting through the open doorway. The roof quickly caught fire, lighting up the entire clearing in an eerie glow. He could see the silhouettes of the Nipmucks and hear their laughing—perhaps they had found rum.

Tamoset had never backed down from another man, and he vowed to kill Poxset if he had the chance. Then his thoughts turned to the children. Killing Englishmen was one thing—it had to be done—but women and children were a different matter. That was not the way a warrior fights, he thought, vowing to take no part in such things.

He stood watching the fire consume the cabin until the roof and walls caved in, leaving nothing but the charred stone chimney standing.

Chapter 11

Tamoset slept fitfully in the woods that night. Now, at dawn, he returned to the village, exhausted. Quietly, he made his way through the small section of the camp where the Wampanoags slept out in the open. A few wigwams had been erected, but sleeping beneath the stars was still comfortable, and there was no great rush to build shelters.

He spotted a large cooking pot hanging over a bed of cold ashes. There was still some stew inside, so he scooped out a bowl, devouring it in seconds. He then found his deerskin blankets and lay down, falling asleep almost instantly.

Ponotuck watched Tamoset through eyes half-closed. He was relieved to see his friend quickly fall asleep. Ponotuck could leave now, before the rest of the village stirred. Stealthily, he picked his way through the slumbering men, grabbed a long bow, and headed southward into the woods.

Another figure silently slipped after him.

Tamoset awoke two hours later, still in a somber and sullen mood. He hoped someday to meet Poxset alone on the trail. To challenge him in camp would surely raise bad blood between the two tribes, thereby weakening the alliance against the English. But the anger burned in his stomach like a hot coal, and he let his mind imagine an encounter with the Nipmuck. Lots of new enemies, thought Tamoset, thinking back on the tall Englishman that had scarred his face. Someday, they will feel my hatred.

He did not welcome the bitterness inside; he wanted to be rid of it for awhile, and decided to go deer hunting. But first, he needed more arrows. He borrowed a large deer antler from a Norwottock brave and walked to the bluff overlooking the river where he gathered chunks of quartz and flint. Holding the stone firmly in one hand, he used the antler in the other to repeatedly strike the stone. Tiny, razer sharp flakes of quartz flew away. He was a fairly skilled toolmaker, and soon a group of children gathered to watch the arrowheads take shape in the hands of the scar-faced Wampanoag from another land.

There was a four-year-old girl in the audience who clapped each time a big flake went flying. Tamoset picked up a long piece of quartz and quickly fashioned a slender feather from it. With great ceremony he looked up at the little girl and handed it to her. The girl beamed with delight.

For the first time Tamoset noticed a woman standing behind the children. When he craned his neck to get a better look, she flashed a smile and then turned away, walking back toward the camp. It was the woman he had seen swimming in the river. He was about to say something, but could not find the words. His eyes watched her go.

Even in that brief look, he felt the same feeling of arousal he had by the river. Her eyes were beautiful, penetrating. This was the first time he had seen her smile, which made her whole face light up. He turned back to his arrowheads, but his concentration wasn't right, and he split the quartz the wrong way.

All he could see was the image of the woman, naked by the mountain stream. He chipped harder.

Later, when five perfectly formed arrowheads lay at his feet, he decided he had more than enough. He prowled the surrounding woods and cut straight, slender hardwood saplings for arrow shafts. The thicker end of the shafts were then notched, and he bound the quartz points inside the notch with deer sinew. Finally, at the tapered end of the shaft he made a notch for the bow string; then he lashed three turkey feathers to the shaft to guide the arrow's flight.

He held the five arrows in his hand and looked them over critically. Not the best he had ever made, but not bad considering how quickly he made them. He then returned the deer antler and set off to hunt.

It was now midday, the worst time to look for game. But Tamoset didn't care; he used the hunt as a reason to be alone. The region to the west of the Connecticut River was hilly, rugged land, largely uninhabited. For centuries it had served as something of a buffer between the Algonquian tribes to the east and the fierce Mohawks who lived to the west. Both peoples used the hills for the fine hunting there, but it was dangerous to do so. Should an Algonquian hunting party run into a band of Mohawks, there could be bloodshed. Lone hunters usually travelled undetected, but every now and then a hunter who entered these hills was never heard from again.

He walked with long strides for seven or eight miles, following a faint game trail which showed promise of fresh deer tracks. At the base of a chestnut tree, he examined the fallen nuts, which were extremely large—a sure sign that a severe winter was coming. Earlier in the year he had noticed how big the blueberries and blackberries had been. He knew that before heavy snow flew, the Creator always made nuts and berries larger than normal so that the birds and animals could survive.

He was glad to see some sign of the Creator. The last few months had shaken Tamoset's faith and left him spiritually confused. Seeing the berries reassured him that the earth's cycles and oneness were still as strong as ever. This terrible war was just a second in the eons of time. He picked a few withered berries, and reflected that there really is no past or future, just the moment.

At the crest of a hill he found an open spot at the edge of a south-facing slope where the warm September sunshine was strongest. Propping his back against a giant white pine, he rested, offering prayers for the safety of his wife and son. He let his mind go free, feeling the power of the trees. The air seemed purer, the silence a comfort. He waited for the voice of his ancestors, waited for a sign. Minutes passed, and he kept his face toward the sun. Thoughts flashed through his mind. The face of Poxset, the Nipmuck who challenged him, appeared. Tamoset wanted revenge against this man, but self-control was everything. To fight Poxset—he knew he could kill him— would only cause friction between the tribes. A soft, raspy voice whispered, "Be strong, your people need you." Then seconds later, "You will be tested." He felt himself floating, the spirits nearby. Minutes or days went by, he couldn't be sure. He tried to concentrate harder, hoping the spirits would assure him that Napatoo and Chusett were well. The sun, however, made him drowsy. He fought the urge to sleep, but the whisper of the breeze in the trees lulled him deeper, and the trance passed into sleep.

* * * *

A half-hour later he was awakened by a noise. A twig snapped nearby. Years of living in the forest had developed Tamoset's hearing to pick up any noise which was not part of the regular wood sounds, even in his sleep. He opened his eyes but remained motionless. If Mohawks were approaching, he figured it best to just lay still; perhaps they would walk right by.

A rustling noise, barely audible, came from the hillside below. Something was definitely there. He stared down the slope, but could see nothing. He waited, his eyes fixed at the spot closest to where the noise came from.

The sound came again. This time, it was followed by the appearance of a black shape. A bear. The creature was upwind of Tamoset, and had no idea the Indian was there. It was preoccupied with its search for grubs, turning over logs with its powerful front legs.

Tamoset sat in awe. The bear was a revered animal to all natives. They believed the bear gave them their wisdom and strength. By eating its heart, they could gain its power. Although the bear was prized for this reason—as well as its fur, fat, teeth and meat—killing the bear was not a simple matter. Silent prayers must first be given to show respect. Legend told them that the bear was actually a spirit form of man. And there were similarities: the bear was extremely protective of its young, was a fierce warrior when aroused, and could walk on two legs.

Tamoset did not want to kill this bear. He was far from camp and could only carry a small portion of the meat back.

But winter was coming, and he knew food would be scarce—besides he could always send others back for the rest of meat. With eyes glued on the beast, he mouthed a prayer of respect for this noble creature.

When the bear put its head down behind a log, Tamoset reached for an arrow. He must have made a noise because the bear suddenly stopped, raising itself on its hind legs to look and smell above the bushes. Its head was enormous. The standing bear made a perfect target, and Tamoset launched the arrow.

The bruin let out a great roar as the arrow buried itself in its chest. Dropping to all fours, the wounded beast went charging and crashing into the forest. The woods echoed with the sound of snapping tree limbs as the enraged bear ran from its unseen attacker.

Tamoset sat still, listening to sounds of destruction caused by the bear's headlong blast through the brush and trees. He would wait a few minutes before following.

After three minutes of running at full steam, the bear slowed to a walk, shaking his head from side to side, spitting up blood. The arrow was causing massive internal bleeding. The bear would eventually tire, lie down and die, never knowing what had happened.

Chapter 12

Ochala looked at the large hunk of bear meat and then stared at Tamoset. He was not used to getting gifts, and the old man was slow to respond. "You killed this bear today?"

"Yes. I was resting by a hillside trail, and when I opened my eyes, the bear was within range of my arrow."

"That is good. The bear and you were destined to be on that hill at the same time." Ochala gestured for Tamoset to join him by his small cooking fire. "So, you did not forget the old canoe-maker by the river?"

Tamoset smiled as he seated himself across the fire. He answered the old man's question with a question of his own. "Oh yes, how could I forget one who spoke as direct as you did?"

Now it was Ochala's turn to smile. Tamoset was surprised—he had thought Ochala was incapable of anything but seriousness. He was going to tell him about the voice he heard, but wondered what the old man would think about someone other than a shaman speaking with the ancestors. Although he sensed Ochala had wisdom, he thought it prudent to limit their initial discussions to the war.

"Tell me, Ochala, do you still think we will lose the war?"

"I'm not so sure now. The whites seem to be fleeing from all their outlying settlements and moving to strong-houses further down the river. I had expected them to fight harder."

Tamoset nodded as he gazed into the orange flames. "They run like dogs. But one thing worries me—we are winning each battle, but we are losing two braves for every English we kill."

Poking the coals, Ochala nodded, "So you noticed that, too." Then he cut a slice of bear meat and stuck it on the roasting stick.

"I think as long as we are driving them from their towns, we shall succeed. They have many muskets, and we cannot help but lose warriors. The one thing we must remember is that it is early; we have only been fighting for three months. And we have planted no crops in that time. Hunger will grip us when the snow flies."

"Yes, I hear many woman talking about going back to their homes before winter sets in. The braves don't like to admit it, but they listen to their women. I'm afraid many will leave before we have taken the town they call Springfield."

Tamoset was startled from his talk by the arrival of a woman. He was even more surprised when he recognized her as the one at the river.

Ochala made the introduction, "This is my daughter, Quinna."

Tamoset's eyes widened. He had seen the two together once before but never made the connection. He thought of that day on the river at the Nipmuck camp. Perhaps she had been helping Ochala with the canoe before she went in the water. The thought of her swimming that day made him uncomfortable, but he couldn't help staring at her.

Quinna did not acknowledge that they had met before, and Tamoset was relieved. She made small talk as she sat down next to her father and turned the roasting stick. "You must miss your home, being so far away," she said. She looked closely at his scar, his eyes.

"Yes, I am an outsider here. We Wampanoags are people of the east. Our land is now crowded with whites." He paused for a second. "It has been difficult; I wonder if my wife and child are safe."

Ochala attempted to reassure him. "I think they are. We would have heard if there were battles to the east."

"Perhaps you will be able to go home soon," added Quinna softly.

Tamoset glanced back at her. He noticed how smooth her copper skin was. Her legs were long and firm.

"Maybe when the trees leaf and the shad run—a long time."

Quinna nodded, then looking at her father said, "I'll get some corn. It is late, you both must be hungry."

She didn't wait for a response but stood and turned toward the wigwam. She knew Tamoset was watching her go. Who was this man, she asked herself? He's different than most. Quieter, no boasting. Seeing him up close allowed her to look beyond his gruesome scar. She thought how his eyes looked like those of someone much older.

For all Quinna's beauty, she spent little time thinking about men. Since the death of her mother eight years ago she was committed to her father; preparing his meals, making his clothes, growing his food and talking with him. She adored him, listening to his stories of the old days, learning of the Creator and hearing his warning of the future. She was at the prime of the marrying age, maybe a little beyond, but the village braves didn't interest her, and her father said the decision to marry was totally her own. This created talk among the villagers, but neither father nor daughter cared.

Tamoset sat talking with Ochala for a couple of minutes longer. Then he surprised the old man by saying, "I must leave now. Enjoy the bear."

As he walked back to the Wampanoag section of camp he thought of Napatoo. I have been away from home too long, he thought; maybe I'll go back for just a couple of days to see if they are safe.

* * * *

The next day, Philip returned to camp after a short trip to Mohawk territory. He was in a foul mood after being rebuffed by the Mohawks. The Mohawks and the Narragansetts were critical of the strength of his alliance, and both were staying out of the conflict. His bitterness, however, could be channelled into action. He went from wigwam to wigwam, campfire to campfire, fanning the flames of hatred against the whites. "Soon," he told the warriors, "we will attack the white soldiers. The river will flow red with their blood. Prepare yourselves for a great battle."

Chapter 13

Tamoset lay hidden on a hillside behind a large hemlock tree. He stole a glance at Philip to his left, noticing the cords of muscle standing out on his friend's neck and jaw. He looked like a cougar ready to pounce. To his right was Ponotuck, whose perspiration was mixing with the blue and red warpaint that streaked his body. They were waiting for a large party of soldiers, under the leadership of Captain Lothrop, to step into an ambush devised by Muttawmp.

The soldiers had recently arrived at Deerfield to carry the season's harvest southward to the more secure town of Hadley. Indian scouts hid themselves all around the town, watching as grain, corn and vegetables were loaded onto carts and wagons. While the troopers were in Deerfield, the main body of warriors felled a number of large trees across the southern trail.

Tamoset shifted his weight to his side, his legs aching from laying in ambush position for so long. He wondered if the soldiers had decided to spend the night in the Deerfield garrison. Maybe this attack is not meant to be, he thought, maybe we are taking on too many soldiers this time. Then, in the distance, he heard horses and the clanging of cutlasses. The soldiers were finally approaching.

When the English first came into view, he was surprised to see that they had put their muskets in the carts that carried the grain. The soldiers were relaxed—after the uneventful march to Deerfield they had let their guard down—and now they were thinking of home. It was a hot, humid day, and some of them were picking grapes alongside the path to slake their thirst. At the fallen trees, they began to bunch up as the progression of wagons was halted.

Tamoset looked at Philip, saw the trace of a smile on his lips, and wondered if he was all right. As tense seconds passed, Tamoset's heart pounded wildly. *What is he waiting for? We have them. Does he think they are too many for us?*

Slowly, Philip bared his teeth, then let out a piercing cry. All at once the Indians let their arrows fly. These were followed by loud cracks from the few muskets they held.

Ten soldiers dropped dead, some falling into a small brook, others slumped over the wagon seats. For an instant, the rest of the column froze in disbelief.

"To your arms!" shouted Captain Lothrop.

A few soldiers got to the muskets and fired off their pieces, but the majority were already running back up the trail to escape the carnage.

Lothrop wheeled his horse about. "Stay together men! Courage!"

A musket ball blew him out of his saddle and into the stream which had now turned crimson from all the English blood.

The scene was pandemonium. The Indians had sealed the rear of the trail, and soldiers were now seeking refuge under the wagons. Others broke for the woods, but three or four Indians went after them, and most were quickly killed.

Upon seeing that the soldiers were pinned down and in disarray, Philip decided to move in. As he stood up, Tamoset caught his arm.

"Wait!" shouted Tamoset. "You don't need to! We can wipe them out from here!"

Philip wrenched his arm free from Tamoset's grip and snarled, "I want to feel them die!"

He made a reckless charge down the hill and leaped onto the back of a wagon. The soldier who was crouched in the driver's seat spun around with his sword. Philip dove through the air, landing with a thud against the white man, both tumbling to the ground. With his left hand, he smashed the soldier's face, and with his right he sank his knife deep into the man's belly.

Another soldier, using his jammed musket as a club charged Philip from the rear. As his musket came swinging down, Philip rolled at the last instant, the blow glancing off his side. With his knife, he slashed at the man's legs, the blade biting deep into flesh. The soldier shrieked in pain, raising his musket to swing again. But Philip was quicker, crashing into him and knocking him backwards. Then, dropping his knife, Philip wrapped his hands around the soldier's throat. His fingers were like a vice, squeezing into the back of the man's neck while his thumbs pushed down on the front, driving the adams apple downward. He watched as the white man's eyes bugged out, then heard his last breath.

All the Indians were pouring off the hillside, emboldened by Philip's daring actions.

The slaughter was over within minutes. Soldiers lay scattered about like so much cordwood. The smell of gun powder hung in the humid air. Indians fanned out searching for valuables or weapons on the dead. The bags of grain were ripped open, the seed mixing with the English blood in the dirt.

Tamoset surveyed the scene. Indians were whooping and laughing at their easy victory. Many young braves were gathered around Philip. He was covered with blood, English blood, and had a maniacal look on his face.

The stories of Philip's bravery would be told and told again. Even though Muttawmp had planned and executed this great victory, Philip was the center of attention.

Chapter 14

John Homer sat at the family table, hunched over his journal, writing by candlelight.

October 2, 1675

Word came today of a terrible disaster at Deerfield. The distressing tidings said that over seventy of our finest young men were cut down at a place being called Bloody Brook.

The war goes poorly. The Indians have the advantage in the Connecticut River Valley and strike at will. Houses are laid in ashes, and wives and children are taken captive. God help us if we do not take the offensive soon.

Elizabeth is worried they will come here next. She talks of taking the children to live with relatives in Boston. At one low point she talked of leaving the country altogether and sailing for England to escape the savage fury.

Perhaps the coming of winter will slow the Indians down. If we can just hang on till spring . . . .   *JGH*

Homer closed his journal and placed it in the trunk kept under the bed. His usual entries were ones that recorded the activities of the farm, such as the size of the harvest, any unusual weather and various planting and harvesting dates. But ever since he fought the natives in the swamp, his thoughts were on the war. And it didn't help that there were wild rumors afloat. Almost weekly it seemed the stories drifted in, most reporting that the Nipmucks and Wampanoags were coming back east, or that the Narragansetts had taken to the war path.

He knew he would never abandon Medfield, but he wondered if maybe Elizabeth and the children should be taken to a more secure town. For the time being, it was a decision he would put off—and hope that the natives could be contained in the western part of the colony. He blew the candle out, banked the fire in the enormous fireplace, and climbed into bed, careful not to wake his wife.

* * * *

The next day he was gathering pumpkins and squash in his field when a neighbor waved from the dirt road that split his land. Not wanting to miss any news, he quickly strode over to where the stone wall met the road.

"What news have ye, Christian?" hollered Homer, approaching his neighbor, who had halted his big chestnut mare.

"I'm afraid the ambush at Deerfield was even worse than we heard. The red devils not only slaughtered all those men, but they now have their weapons and all that food which was being transported," said Christian Leverett, shaking his head slowly as if in disbelief.

Homer put his foot up on the stone wall and lit his pipe. " 'Tis only a matter of time until they attack Springfield, and who knows where they go next."

"Aye, that's the truth, John. I'm writing to the Governor and asking that troops be sent to Medfield. I fear the Indians will be heading our way."

Homer took a deep draw from the clay pipe, then watched the smoke curl up and away into the clear autumn sky. Beyond his field the trees were in a glorious display of vivid reds, oranges and yellows. But he scarcely noticed, worried that natives might be lurking in the area, and knowing that securing more troops was a long shot.

Wiping his dirty brow, Homer looked directly at Leverett, and shook his head. "The governor is too busy wringing his hands, wondering what to do; we shan't see any troops." Then in a more sarcastic voice he added, "Besides, haven't you heard? Our leaders say God is punishing us for too much drink and play! They never mention how some of our richer citizens cheated the Indians year after year."

Leverett frowned, "Careful, John. It's all right to speak your mind with me, but don't let the others hear you talk like that."

Homer knew he was right, but his frustration had been building with word of each new defeat on the warfront.

"I wonder how long it will take us to change our tactics and really go after the Indians. It takes us days to follow their trail after they raid a town."

"You'll hear no argument from me," said Leverett. "I've heard some of our folks call the Indians cowards because they won't meet us in open battle. Why should they? We keep falling into their ambushes. Sooner or later we will listen to that Ben Church and begin fighting more like the Indians and less like bloody fools."

Homer nodded. He, too, had heard all about Ben Church, and knew that Church alone had a plan that could bring victory.

"I'm sick of waiting, sick of worrying that Philip's braves are getting closer. This farm is all I have. I say we go after them—no matter what the cost—and destroy him and his warriors before the snow comes."

The men talked a while more, both wondering if their farms would still be standing in the spring.

Homer put his pipe away and motioned to his field. "Reckon, I better get back to it—we may need every one of those pumpkins before this winter is through."

Chapter 15

A bone-chilling wind swept up the Connecticut River valley, and Tamoset wrapped himself more tightly in his beaver-skin cloak. It was only early November, but the last two weeks had felt like the dark months of January. He sat cross-legged with the other warriors gathered around a great fire. Tonight, Philip would address the assembled representatives and unveil his plans.

The attacks along the Connecticut River had come to a close with a successful raid on Springfield and a stand-off at Hatfield. It was unclear what would happen next, but Tamoset had heard much talk of tribes returning to their winter quarters. Some families had already slipped out of the large encampment and returned to more familiar territory. For the first time, Tamoset allowed himself to be hopeful that he would soon see Napatoo and little Chusett.

A hush fell over the crowd when they spotted Philip coming. He strode into the center of the ring where the fire shone on his impressive features. All the village was aware of his daring actions at Bloody Brook. Some estimated that he had killed five English that day, all with his bare hands.

Philip seemed not to notice the icy wind, even though he was clothed only in ankle-high moccasins, a breech cloth and his distinctive colorful belt of beads. He let the anticipation mount by slowly walking around the circle nodding at those he recognized. Then he raised his arm and all eyes were on him.

"Friends, warriors!" shouted Philip, splitting the night air. "It is good so many of you have come. I called you here to acknowledge your great victories and acts of courage!"

A great cheer went up and braves raised both hands high with clenched fists. Some stood up and drew knives and stabbed wildly at imaginary enemies. They screamed for the joy of it; their hearts swelled with pride. Revenge had given them back their self-esteem. They had finally turned the tables on the English, who seemed totally helpless to stop them.

Philip again raised his hand, this time to restore order.

"We have hurt the English badly. We have forced them to flee their farms. Now they hide in garrisons, like rabbits in a hole." He paused and then thundered louder than ever, "But we are not yet finished! We must drive every last one of them out of this valley!"

There were grunts of approval from some, but no wild cheering. Some braves kept quiet. It was clear they had come to celebrate, not to plan new battles.

Philip continued, his eyes showing fiercely in the firelight. "Yes, we must kill more. Do not let the snow stop our progress. If we rest, the whites will strengthen. They must be driven from the Great River before the next growing season. We will need to plant our crops here, or we will have no food. I would rather die fighting now than to watch hunger come later!"

Grumbling was heard—they had been on the warpath for months; winter was for resting.

Philip was stunned by the dissent. His facial muscles tightened, and he clenched his teeth.

Tamoset watched him closely, afraid his friend might lose control. He knew his rage could be like that of a wounded bear, and he thought Philip might pounce on a Nipmuck who was particularly loud in his muttering. He thought this might be the turning point he secretly feared, wondered if Philip, or any man for that matter, could control such a group.

"Listen to me!" snarled Philip. "We are winning this war! Do not stop till we have completed what we have started! The arrow has left the bow!"

His voice was raspy from shouting. He paused, slowly walking around the circle, using the time to get control of himself, letting his words sink in. He seemed to look each brave in the eye. It was so quiet that the crackling of the fire could be heard.

Philip stopped his pacing. The rage seemed to leave his face, and a calm, almost faraway look took its place.

"Can't you see we must kill all the whites?" his voice was restrained, his hands open. "Do you think they will sit idly by after so much bloodshed? Do you think they will make peace? No! They are hanging our people in Boston. Others are being put on great boats and sent out to sea."

Again he paused, this time looking into the fire, rather than into the crowd. Firelight danced across his face, giving him an unearthly look. Tamoset wondered if the Spirit was whispering to him, giving him the words to say, and a chill ran down his spine.

Every eye was watching Philip, wondering what he would say next. Seconds passed, and some of the braves shifted uncomfortably, but Philip still stared into the fire, as if he were alone, as if the flames were his only friends. Then he looked up, not at the warriors before him, but over their heads, to the east, toward the land of his ancestors.

When he addressed them again, his voice was soft, so soft the braves had to lean forward to hear. "There is no future for us except death if we do not succeed. We cannot rest. We are warriors. Walk tall as trees and be strong like mountain, and victory will come."

There was now a murmur of approval. His words had their intended effect. Being reminded of the consequences of failure gave the braves something new to ponder. The sheer power and emotion in their leader's voice had made them think anew.

Philip knew he had struck the right cord. He left the fire and walked into the night.

Muttawmp and other leaders got up and echoed Philip's words. Slowly, with each new speech, the warriors worked themselves back up to a renewed frenzy. The celebratory atmosphere returned.

Someone grabbed a drum, and others started the dance of war. When all the lesser sachems had spoken, women and children gathered round the great fire to join the impromptu festival of unity.

Tamoset watched the scene as a spectator would watch a game. He could hardly believe Philip had convinced the warriors to press the fight. But watching the wild dancing, he wondered how long so large and fragmented a group could be held together.

* * * *

"So here you are, my quiet friend!" exclaimed Ponotuck, slapping Tamoset on the back.

Tamoset spun around; he had not seen his friend in days.

Ponotuck gave a wide, toothy grin. With one hand he pushed his long flowing hair out of his eyes, and with the other he offered a jug to Tamoset.

"Oh no," said Tamoset, shaking his head, "I've seen what that does to men."

"Yes, it does do something. Something good. It makes men feel strong, happy. Haven't we had enough hard times? Why not feel the power of this firewater in your veins?"

"Where did you get it?"

"I bought it from a Nipmuck. He took it from a home in Deerfield—just after he scalped the greedy farmer! Look around you, Tamoset. Others are enjoying the taste of fire."

It was true. Tamoset could see another jug being passed among a group of laughing Nipmucks.

"Here, take a swallow," said Ponotuck, swinging the bottle into Tamoset's hands.

He hesitated, then took a sip, feeling the liquor burn a slow path down his throat and into his stomach. The warmth of the rum felt good, immediately eliminating the chill of the November air. He raised the jug to his lips again, this time filling his mouth with the sweet-tasting liquid before swallowing.

"You will feel much better, now," said Ponotuck.

He did. In fact, he felt like smiling for the first time in months. "Let's walk around, visit with the others," suggested Tamoset.

Ponotuck grinned—the normally restrained Tamoset was suddenly social.

First they stopped at a group of Nipmucks who also had rum. They were gathered around a small fire, away from the central celebration. Some of the Nipmucks knew Tamoset by the scar on his face, and it seemed everyone knew Ponotuck.

"Come, join us in drink!" shouted a Nipmuck, who was already quite drunk. He passed the jug to Ponotuck who took a long pull, then passed it on to Tamoset.

Tamoset thought it would be rude not to accept their hospitality, and he too took a hefty drink. He heard a ringing in his ears that was not unpleasant. Then he settled down on deer skins spread around the fire, listening to the Nipmucks talk about a soldier they found hiding up in a tree during the battle of Bloody Brook.

"We shot him with six arrows before he finally fell," said a Nipmuck. "And even when he dropped he still wasn't dead. I had to knock him with my club."

The jug passed around the group again. Tamoset was now outright drunk. He wondered why he had not spent more time with these Nipmucks before; they were certainly friendly.

Ponotuck started to tell stories of his bravery at Bloody Brook. He explained how he had charged into the whites, splitting the head of a soldier who was about to fire at Philip.

Tamoset smiled. Ponotuck didn't do anything extraordinary at the battle. In fact, he recalled that his friend spent most of the battle behind the safety of a large beech tree. But Tamoset was in too good a mood to ruin Ponotuck's story.

Minutes later the aroma of a nearby cooking fire was carried on a puff of breeze. All of a sudden Tamoset realized he was ravenous and excused himself from the group.

"Wait, take one more drink," said a Nipmuck, grabbing Tamoset's arm. "You are quiet, but we know you got that scar in battle. You deserve more rum."

Tamoset took a another swig, and went reeling into the night. It seemed the whole camp was out and about. Some people were still aroused from Philip's speech, celebrating in advance all the future victories that would soon be won.

"Tamoset, is that you?" said a woman's voice from behind.

He spun around and almost fell. Squinting, he carefully stepped toward where he heard the voice.

Quinna stepped out of the darkness. "I knew that was you. Why did you not eat with my father? He may be gruff, but he likes you."

Tamoset had never seen such beauty in his life. She was standing next to him now, smiling. His mind raced. Again he thought of that day he caught her bathing in the river. The vision of her standing naked was vividly etched in his mind.

He looked into her eyes. They seemed larger than ever and more inviting.

"You are so beautiful," he said in a husky whisper. And then, without thinking, he pulled her towards him and kissed her.

She quickly pulled away. "No," she said, holding him off at arms length. "This is not right."

For a second she stared at him, then turned and ran, disappearing into the night.

The power of the rum suddenly left his body and he felt sick. He knew he had made a terrible blunder. "What's happening to me?" he whispered weakly, thinking of Napatoo.

For a long time he stood in the same spot. His mind raced in confusion. For a minute he considered following Quinna, but instead walked to his sleeping skins. He lay down, looking at the stars, and then, thankfully, sleep came.

Chapter 16

The first hint of grey light filtered through the night mist which rose from the river and enveloped the camp. Drums and turtle rattles lay where they were dropped, and only the dull roar of the falls could be heard.

Sleep would not come to Philip. He walked alone, quietly passing the wigwams, then picking his way past a few Wampanoag men, who lay covered in furs, sleeping out in the open. These were his most seasoned warriors, who had not yet got around to building winter wigwams. He looked down and saw Tamoset, easily identified by his facial scar. Next to him lay Ponotuck, snoring loudly. They must have tasted much rum last night, he thought disgustedly.

As Philip turned to go something shiny caught his eye. He squatted next to Ponotuck and looked more closely. It was an English coin, sticking out of the dirt. He picked it up, scraping the soil beneath it. More coins appeared, as well as a large quantity of wampum.

Blood rose to his face in anger. All money plundered by the braves was to have been turned over to the sachems to buy muskets and powder from the French. For a second he stood still, his mind racing, questions quickly answered. At first he did not want to believe it, but the pieces of the puzzle all fit, and a tremor of rage passed through him.

"Get up, you snake!" he roared, kicking the slumbering Ponotuck.

Ponotuck groaned and staggered to his feet. Tamoset and the other braves were awakened by the commotion. They were staring at Philip, wondering what was wrong.

"Philip!" cried Ponotuck, pulling the hair back from his eyes. "For a moment I thought it was the English!" Philip's stare sent a chill down Ponotuck's spine. "What is it?" asked Ponotuck taking a step backward.

Philip didn't move or speak, but his eyes had a wild look. Then he held out his hand with the coins in it.

Ponotuck's eyes widened, a flicker of fear passing over them. He quickly looked down at his sleeping area and saw the pile of wampum and coins which Philip had dug up.

"I, I found those at a farm house, I've been meaning to give them to you."

"You're lying!" screamed Philip.

"No, no. Listen to me, Philip!" pleaded Ponotuck.

But Philip shook his head slowly. A trace of a cruel smile formed on his lips, and he stepped forward, hand moving toward his belt and tomahawk.

Ponotuck bolted. He sprinted over sleeping bodies with Philip right behind him. He might have made it had not one of the warriors he jumped over grabbed his legs, sending him crashing to the ground. Philip leaped on his back, and with a vicious swing, buried his tomahawk in Ponotuck's skull.

Tamoset watched in horror as his friend's head cracked open like a ripe melon. He could not believe this was happening, tried to cry out but no words came.

Philip kicked the lifeless body. "Traitor!" he thundered. Then he stormed away, leaving everyone shocked and reeling, wondering why.

* * * *

It wasn't until later that day that Tamoset approached Philip, who was sitting by the river, staring out at the dark water sliding toward the falls. Tamoset stopped ten feet away and just waited. His head hurt from the rum, and he felt a black cloud of despair like he had never known.

When Philip didn't acknowledge him he spoke. "Why?" was all he said.

Philip looked at him, his face ashen, but showing no emotion. "Haven't you put it together, my friend?" asked Philip, running a hand through his hair.

Tamoset shook his head painfully, thinking of Ponotuck. "No, I don't understand, I don't understand at all. He could have been punished, you didn't have to kill him for hiding the money."

"I would not have, if that's all it was. Don't you see, Ponotuck was a traitor. Think of all the times he mysteriously dissappeared. Think of all the questions he asked. Remember when we were fleeing from the swamp and heading towards the Nipmucks? Ponotuck arrived with a sheep he said he took from a farm. Later that day, we were attacked by Mohegans who somehow knew where we were."

Tamoset cocked his head, remembering the surprise attack that almost got them killed.

"Yes," said Philip wearily, "it was Ponotuck who must have told them. I have long known there was a traitor among us, and lately I've been watching Ponotuck. Just recently I saw him slip off in the early morning, and thought it odd that he would go hunting alone. I know now that he was not hunting, he was selling information to the English."

Tamoset was about to say it was guesswork, that Philip could not be sure. But what good would it do? Ponotuck was dead.

A crow gave its mournful "Caw, caw" from the top of a nearby pine, seemingly mocking the men, mocking the blood on their hands. It was cold, the trees bare, and winter was on the doorstep. Tamoset shuddered involuntarily. He had many things to say, and he knew now was the time because they were alone. "We should ... ," he started to say, but his voice trailed off. Philip looked at him, waited, then turned back toward the river, saying nothing.

The two men stood staring at the dark waters. They were silent for a long time. Finally Tamoset said, "We should move the camp."

Philip nodded, "Braves will use this as an excuse to leave."

Tamoset thought it time to head eastward. He had heard other warriors talking of going to winter camp with the Narragansetts. Maybe now he would be with Napatoo before the snow flies. But Philip said nothing more and stood up with a sigh.

"Wait, Philip. Don't you miss your wife and son? Don't you miss our land, the smell of the ocean?"

Philip spun around, glaring at his friend. "Of course I do! Do you think I am without feeling? Do you think I don't worry about my wife? I know the men are tired—so am I. But we can't let the English rest. Do you think we can just stop a war because it is cold? The easy way is the path to failure."

Tamoset knew Philip was right. And despite everything that had happened he could not abandon him at this critical time.

Philip's voice softened, "Maybe we should split the camp."

Tamoset jerked his head back, taken by surprise, "What do you mean?"

"We have to let the English know we are strong. And we need to show other tribes that we can strike whenever and wherever we want. Maybe then they will join. So far the only real damage we have done is here along the Great River. I think it's time to move the fight toward Boston. When the Narragansetts see how easily we burn town after town they will fight. Then by the planting moon we will attack Boston and Plymouth. The English will either get in their boats and leave or make peace on our terms."

Caught up in Philip's vision, Tamoset gripped his friend by the arm. "Yes, yes, there are many towns we can easily burn. The soldiers won't know where we will strike next. If we leave some warriors here in the west and some go east, we will burn twice as many houses."

Philip smiled, "We will take half the men and go to Wachusett. From there we will launch our raids. Soon we will be spilling English blood in Wampanoag country."

Wachusett, meaning "by the great hill" in the Algonkian tongue, lay just forty-five miles northwest of Boston, and there were many English towns in the vicinity. It was a bold move, a gamble really, putting the tribe at risk, but at the same time it would bring the warriors close to the heart of the enemy.

Tamoset didn't say it, but part of his excitement was that he would be closer to the Narragansett camp. Maybe he could later convince Philip that another meeting with Canonchet was worthwhile —then he would see Napatoo and Chusett.

* * * *

An hour later Muttawmp had agreed to Philip's plan. Half the warriors would travel eastward, and half would stay in the west. Scouts would be posted to protect the group that stayed on the river from a surprise attack. They had debated whether or not Ponotuck had told the English where they were or if he had just warned them of upcoming Indian attacks. Some elders openly wondered if Ponotuck really had been a traitor—maybe he really did get the silver from the farmhouses.

In the end it was decided that even if the English knew where the camp was they did not have the numbers to launch an offensive. Surely the settlers of the Connecticut River valley were just trying to survive. Springfield lay in ruins, Hatfield was still reeling from repeated raids, provisions had been destroyed, and bitterly cold temperatures would make it all but impossible for white men to take to the trail.

Tamoset was glad to be leaving, but there was one last thing to do. He wanted to say goodby to Ochala. He wondered if Quinna had told Ochala about the incident when he was drunk. I must find out, he thought. But inside he knew it was only justification for seeing her one last time.

Quinna saw him approaching from across the camp and stayed seated when he stood opposite the cooking fire. It's good Ochala's not here, she thought, maybe now I can find out what his intentions are.

She said nothing, letting him stand there awkwardly.

"I came to say goodbye," said Tamoset nervously. He couldn't bring himself to say he was sorry. What could he say—that the rum made him do it?

"We might see each other by Wachusett," she said in a flat voice.

Tamoset had never considered that she too might go east.

Quinna read the look on his face, "Don't be surprised. The other night you acted like you wanted to see me ... often."

She was probing him, looking for a reaction. But Tamoset only looked into the small fire, watching whiffs of smoke get carried on the breeze. His brow was furrowed, and it looked like he might leave.

She decided to ease up. "Wachusett is no farther from our homeland than here. Ochala is talking to Muttawmp about it now."

She was about to continue, but she noticed two old women sitting at the next cooking fire listening to every word. She did not want village talk to get back to Ochala. As it was, most of the tribe already made her a topic of conversation, often starting wild rumors. Why hadn't she married? Did she think she was too good for even the best braves? Was she evil; did she talk to spirits?

The younger girls were jealous of her looks and figure, and all the men were aware whenever she walked by. Quinna had a presence that could not be ignored, and she possessed a sensuality that filled some married women with hate because they knew their husbands lusted after her. Poxset, in particular, had made his desires known.

On top of all this she was strong-willed and highly protective of her father, who was an outspoken and controversial member of the tribal council. No, she did not need word to get around that there was something between her and this strange Wampanoag warrior.

She stood up, looked squarely at Tamoset and said, "I hope your wife and child are fine. Be safe." And with that she turned and went into the wigwam.

* * * *

The next day Tamoset and the other Wampanoags crossed the river and headed east. He had no idea if Quinna was with the 300 Nipmucks who were following.

Chapter 17

December 9, 1675

Much snow has fallen and it has been bitter cold for days on end.

This may be my last entry. We are planning to attack the Narragansetts. Tommorrow I leave to join men from Connecticut, Rhode Island and Plymouth to march on the swamp fortress. It is said there are over a thousand Narragansetts living there as well as many of Philip's men. Although the Narragansetts profess their peacefulness, we think they are hiding the enemy. We cannot let them rest and grow strong over the winter only to cause great mischief in the spring.

Plymouth's General Winslow will lead our army, and I am much heartened to hear that Benjamin Church will be at his side. Still, I pray to the Almighty to watch over Elizabeth and the children, and if it is in His plan, to bring me back in one piece.

JGH

Fifteen other Medfield volunteers gathered with Homer at dawn and began the long march southward. They made good time and met more soldiers at Attleboro, where they planned to spend the night.

General Winslow was there, and with the men gathered round he addressed the troops:

"Men, I promise you this: if we take the fort and drive the enemy out of Narragansett country, you will each receive a gratuity of land besides your promised wages."

A great cheer went up—land was what started this war, and land was what it was all about. Some of the men would have followed Winslow straight to hell, if they were offered land for the trip.

Winslow let the men calm down; then he tried to build their courage and optimism:

"It will be a difficult march and tough battle, but now that the leaves are off the trees the heathen will have no place to hide. These Pagans are harboring the enemy, and they must be destroyed. 'Tis dangers aplenty, but I know we are up to it."

Homer listened to the little speech and muttered to the man next to him, "Danger aplenty? Why doesn't he just tell the truth—half of us won't be going home at all. I've already fought the redskins once in a swamp, and believe me, the carnage will be awful."

His partner had just left the tavern to hear Winslow's talk, and he still held a wooden tankard of ale. "John, if you're right, and I reckon you are, you best enjoy all the comforts possible before we march. Come on, I'll buy you an ale, and we'll spend our last warm night toasting to the death of our red King, Philip."

The next morning they marched to Seekonk. They were ferried across the Seekonk River, then proceeded south to Wickford, Rhode Island. This was the designated rendezvous for all the militias, including the Connecticut men who arrived with a small contigenent of Mohegans.

Winslow sent Captain Moseley, Benjamin Church and a large number of troops out into the surrounding countryside to scout for natives. They could see no evidence of the rumored swamp fort, but did find isolated groups of natives foraging in the woods for food.

Some of the soldiers were mounted on horseback and it wasn't difficult to capture the natives. The women, children, and a few of the younger braves were immediately shipped back to Boston to be sold for slavery. The remaining braves were beheaded in front of the cheering troops.

Over the next few days, this scene was to repeat itself—no fort could be found, just a scattering of skirmishes and a few captured natives. But on the morning of December 18th, a brave was captured who spoke English. As he was about to be beheaded, he screamed out, "I show you fort!" A stunned Moseley stopped the execution, and he and Benjamin Church interrogated the man for an hour.

His name was Peter, and he had lived amongst the English until recently. He described a four-acre patch of dry land in the middle of a place called the Great Swamp which was surrounded by a palisade of spiked logs. He called it a winter camp, where the Indians protected themselves from blasts of icy wind and ravenous wolves. The only way into the camp was on a single log that crossed over a surrounding ditch.

Captain Winslow, still pale from a fever, was inside the garrison when Ben Church came running in. "Beg pardon, Captain, tremendous news! We know where the fort is!"

Winslow looked up from the letter he was writing, "What? You've found the fort?"

"We haven't found it, but we know how to get there. We captured a Christian Indian, and he told us all about it. He says he even knows how to get us inside."

"Do you trust this devil?" said Winslow, rubbing his blood-shot eyes.

"Yes, he described a large winter camp, very similar to what I've heard from other Indians."

"Well, I'm not so sure." Winslow nervously scratched his beard. "But we havn't got much choice. Provisions are running out, and I'm worried about desertion. Tell Moseley to get the men ready at once; we march south in an hour."

* * * *

Inside the sprawling winter camp, row upon row of wig-wams stretched from one side of the palisade to the next. Roughly a thousand natives lived here, mostly women, children and old men, along with a few braves. The bulk of the Narra-gansett warriors were assembled just a few miles away waiting for Canonchet to decide the next move.

The English had been pressuring Canonchet to give up any Wampanoags he was protecting, but that was unthinkable to the great sachem. Yet, still he held out hope that his people could avoid this conflict, and he planned to continue his ongo-ing dialogue with Roger Williams.

Napatoo was one of the Wampanoags living inside the winter camp. She sat on a bedframe in a wigwam watching Chusett play with a small rattle. Bags of corn, beans and groundnuts lay in a U-shape around the perimeter of the wig-wam. Wild onions and herbs hung from the roof pole. Deer, beaver and bear skins lay on the floor and the bedframes. A tiny cooking fire in the center of the wigwam gave it a cozy feeling.

She never tired of looking at Chusett. Everyday brought new and wonderful changes in the child's development, and lately she began to see a resemblance between him and Tamoset. Would the boy have a chance to know his father, she wondered?

Napatoo had not seen Tamoset in five months. Various warriors who had visited the camp told her that they had seen him and he was fine. But she knew he would be fighting by Philip's side, making him a prime target.

Philip! Why did he start this terrible bloodshed? We were fine living on Montaup, she reasoned. Now I'm separated from Tamoset, and we live as guests of a strange tribe. And rumors circulate daily that a large body of soldiers is marching south into Narragansett country.

More braves will die, men who should be enjoying the prime of their life and teaching our children the Wampanoag ways. Philip and his quest for power caused this. He should have been like Canonchet and talked with the English, learned to live with them and traded with them.

In spite of the talk of soldiers coming, Napatoo felt relatively safe. She remembered the walk into this swamp island, and knew that the whites would never find their way through so many miles of thick brush and trees which grew out of the ooze and on the hummucks. And travel would be especially difficult this winter with temperatures so severe that even some of the swamp springs were freezing.

If the whites entered the swamp, they would surely get lost, and the bitter cold would drive them back to their square houses. Still, she was glad the Narragansetts took extra precautions, cutting down the trees around the camp so that their branches pointed outward, forming an impenetrable tangle.

Napatoo tried not to think of these threats, and instead did her best to repay the kindness shown to her by the Narragansetts. Daily she ground corn in the rock mortar, then mixed it with dried blueberries, cranberries, water and beaver fat. The mixture was patted into dough cakes; then it was cooked on a flat stone over the fire. On other days she made wooden and clay bowls for the tribe or sewed winter leggings and deerskin cloaks. She could help in her own way.

* * * *

"Napatoo, some of us are gathering in Weesaka's lodge. Bring your sewing. Chusett can play with the other children." It was Nippeniket, the large Narragansett woman who shared her wigwam with Napatoo. The two had formed a close friendship.

Tall and powerful Nippeniket and slight Napatoo made an unusual twosome when walking about the camp. They were constantly talking, and this bond had been the major reason Napatoo had kept up her spirit through the last few months.

Nippeniket shared Napatoo's view that fighting the English would only cause endless bloodshed. She had once encountered white people while digging clams and had tried to communicate with them using a kind of sign language. The Englishwomen were dressed in black and talked using grunting sounds which were unintelligible. Yes they were ugly, and yes they looked sickly, but they seemed to mean no harm.

Napatoo had never spoken with whites and had only seen them at a distance. She knew the Narragansetts had more frequent encounters with the English, and she recognized their neutrality as a hopeful sign that the two peoples could live together.

Since coming to the Narragansett camp she had heard much talk of a white man called Roger Williams. Whenever an Englishman or an Indian committed a serious infraction, Canonchet would call on this Roger Williams, and they would agree to punish the instigator. Surely, thought Napatoo, the whites of Plymouth must have such a man who has the power to punish the whites who were settling on Wampanoag land.

Napatoo looked up from her work, pushing long strands of hair off her forehead and back into place, "Yes, it will be good to see the others. Without brothers and sisters, Chusett needs to be with the other children. I'm spoiling him—he's got to learn how to be with other boys and girls."

"When Tamoset comes, he will hardly know Chusett. He will be the proud father."

"Oh yes, Tamoset was always picking up Chusett and talking to him. He had already made him a little bow and arrow!"

Napatoo lifted the child and put him in the pack that was hanging from the side of the wigwam. Then she stopped and gave Nippeniket a sideways glance. "Why did you say when Tamoset comes?"

Nippeniket laughed her booming laugh, "I was wondering when you would ask! Rumors say that the Wampanoags and some of the Nipmucks are moving from their camp on the

Great River and many are coming toward the rising sun—per-haps Tamoset will find his way here before too long."

Napatoo tried to contain herself, but her eyes began to tear with a joyful hope.

Chapter 18

"Wake up, John, time to move out." It was five in the morning, and Benjamin Church was going from man to man, rousing them before daylight.

Homer grunted, straightening his stiff legs. He had slept in a fetal position to retain warmth. His cap and blanket were covered with snow, and he couldn't feel his frozen feet inside his boots. He lay alongside 1,000 other men who also spent a miserable night trying to sleep in an open field. All were exhausted from the previous afternoon's rapid march to this forlorn place south of Wickford, just at the fringe of the white settlements.

Church came back to Homer, squatting down next to him. "John, I'm going to need your help; one of the men died during the night, and I want to move the body to the rear before too many of the men see it."

"It's no wonder; I shan't be surprised if we find another dead. I could hear some of the men hacking through the night. And this snow doesn't help," he said, squinting into the falling flakes.

"I know. The Plymouth men are especially ill-prepared. Half of them don't have blankets, and there isn't a biscuit left among the lot of them."

Homer rubbed his feet trying to restore circulation. "I'll wager Winslow slept quite warmly in the house yonder, and is having a big breakfast to boot," he said, referring to Winslow's rather large girth. Then continuing, "I hope he's as good a soldier as he is politician—to him this mission is just another opportunity for personal fame."

Church winked, "I know; he knows nothing about the Indians, but so far he's done a good job heeding my advice. He listens closely, then makes it sound like my suggestions were his own ideas."

Homer managed a weak smile. The two men had become quick friends on the trail. Church had sent word out that anyone who had experience fighting Indians should report to him at once. Over 200 men presented themselves, and from those he picked 50 to march as detail with General Winslow.

When he learned that Homer had been involved in a previous swamp fight, he introduced himself, and the two men discussed tactics and strategy. They soon learned each had been involved in separate ambushes during the first few days of the war.

Benjamin Church was something of a legend to the settlers of Massachusetts and Plymouth Bay Colony. The story of how he had saved his men from an attack by a large group of natives was made all the more legendary because he ran into gunfire to retrieve his fallen hat. Some thought he did this to gain fame by showing courage, but those that knew him said that he simply liked that particular hat.

He was a strong advocate for fighting like the natives, taking the battle to the field rather than waiting to be attacked. Having spent much time in the woods, he was an expert tracker and marksman, making it a point to learn the ways of the forest from native friends.

He was acquainted with many of the Indian sachems, and he urged the Plymouth Colony leaders to open a dialogue with the neutral natives before they went to Philip's side. In the first couple of months of the war, he was ignored by the Plymouth hierarchy, but now, with the war going poorly, the leaders began to listen.

* * * *

Once all the men had been awakened, Mosley and the native guide Peter led the way into the swamp. Homer was behind Church and Winslow in a single-file line that snaked its way through the frozen swamp. The path that Peter led them on was wide enough for only one person to pass, and branches clawed at the men's faces. It was difficult to see more than a few feet ahead, and the deeper they went into the swamp, the more nervous Homer became. Try as he might, he could not stop thinking of the terrible results of his first swamp foray.

It was too late for any desertions—the men had no idea where to run to, and the path they were on was apparently the only way out of the swamp. Most of the men simply wanted to get the fight over with, so they could get back to the garrison at Warwick for food and shelter. The cold had a way of taking the passion and courage out of even the most disciplined soldier.

Homer walked with hunched shoulders, seeing only the tracks left by the man in front. Blinding snow stung his eyes. The wind howled above the trees and tore at his tattered scarf and mittens. His skin was so dry and frigid, he thought his face would crack like glass. Despite his pain, he worried about what lay ahead—what if they had underestimated the Narragansett's numbers?

A particularly strong blast of bone-rattling wind almost knocked him off his feet, and he wondered how the men would fight after such a march. He passed one man sitting on the frozen ice begging and sobbing that he couldn't go on. The line of soldiers passed him by, without so much as a word. Each man was concentrating on his own situation; most were just trying to put one foot in front of the other.

Homer snapped his head up—a musket blast from the front of the line! Then more gunshots.

"Let's go, John!" It was Church, always wanting to be in the action.

They struggled up the path to the front of the column where Moseley was kneeling in the snow. He looked and pointed ahead.

"They're lurking about. Just exchanged fire with a few of the devils, but they slipped away. For a moment I thought our friend here led us into an ambush," said Moseley gesturing toward the Indian guide Peter.

Church turned to Peter, "How much farther?"

"We close. Big camp over there."

Homer peered ahead, but with the snow coming down almost horizontally all he could see were a few shadowy trees.

"Well, they know we're coming now," said Homer in a grim voice.

Moseley stood, priming his gun and placing a rag over the powder to keep the snow from getting it wet. "We best move fast; no sense giving them time to prepare." He grabbed Peter by the neck, hissing, "And if you're lying, I'll take your head off, then carve you into quarters."

They moved farther up the icy trail, with Peter leading the way. A few minutes later a shot rang out, and the soldier standing behind Peter keeled over.

"Take cover!" shouted Church.

Moseley yanked Peter by the hair and drew his sword.

"You swine! You're leading us to a trap!"

"No, no!" screamed Peter, pointing ahead. "The camp, the camp! Look!"

From behind the safety of a tree, Homer squinted his ice-encrusted eyes. Through the snow and trees he could barely make out the outline of a wall. The fort!

Natives were firing from behind the palisade, taking advantage of the slight elevation of their swamp island. Church dodged the whizzing musket balls and ran to Moseley's side.

"It would be suicide for us to charge!"

Moseley was shaking his head, about to order the assault, when Peter shouted, "This way, this way! Fort not finished!"

They followed him without the slightest hesitation, now that they knew he was telling the truth. Within three or four minutes they were at the back of the fort where there was a partial opening in the wall. A single log crossed a five foot gully of ice which stretched along the edge of the island camp.

Church turned to Homer, shouting, "Go get Winslow!"

Homer raced back along the line, men grabbing at him asking what was happening ahead. He saw Winslow, doing his best with his fat frame to move quickly forward. The General was well aware of the talk that would ensue if he left all the decisions to Moseley.

"Where's Moseley, where's Church!" he rasped between gulps of air.

"Up ahead sir—we found an opening in the fort, but there's only one log that crosses the ditch!"

Homer helped Winslow to the front where Moseley and Church were trading fire with the natives behind the stockade.

Winslow immediately grasped the danger of the situation, but still ordered the assault—making sure he wasn't part of it. He ordered two companies to charge the fort, while the rest would try to keep the natives pinned down with musket fire.

When the first soldiers reached the log, the natives concentrated all their shooting there. Musket balls and arrows found their mark, and soldiers toppled from the log into the ditch, like apples falling from a tree. The officers sent more soldiers forward, hoping that the natives would retreat when they saw how many English were going to swarm across. But the results were the same. The ditch turned crimson with the blood from dozens of dead and wounded, stacked on top of each other below the log.

Church sprang up to go with the forward company, but Winslow would have none of it, hollering, "Church! Stay back, I want you here for counsel!"

"We can't keep this up; the men are totally exposed on that log!"

Winslow conferred with Moseley, and the two decided that Moseley should lead the next charge. Church knew it was futile to argue, so instead he tried a new approach.

"Let me take Homer and a few good men and attack the fort from another side! We can create a diversion long enough for you and some men to get across the log and establish themselves!"

Moseley didn't wait for Winslow to respond, "Yes, yes, that will work! We'll make our charge when we hear your muskets."

Church, Homer and a few others slipped away from the main group, fighting their way through the deep snow and tangles of brush to the opposite side of the island camp. Silently they made their way to the palisade wall where they could peer between the standing logs. All they could see were the outline of a few wigwams immediately in front of where they stood.

Church motioned for the men to gather around. "Listen boys, I'll fire a shot to let the devils know we're here, but I want the rest of you to hold your fire until you have a target. It shouldn't take more than a few seconds for some braves to come running. Take good aim and make your shots count."

Then Church turned to Homer, "Right after you shoot, we run back to Winslow and Moseley, I think the men will get over the log this time, and I want to be with them when they do."

Homer nodded in agreement, his heart racing. He took his mittens off and with frozen, shaking fingers loaded his musket while the other men did the same. For some reason he suddenly thought of his wife, could even see her face, and wondered if that meant it was his day to die.

He said a silent prayer; he was terrified to die in this frozen swamp, and his shaking intensified. Church was next to him, loading, and Homer stole a glance at him. He envied his calmness and hoped his friend did not notice how bad his nerves had become.

When everyone was ready they stuck the ends of their musket barrels through the cracks in the wall. Then Church fired.

Within seconds they could see the shadowy figures of six or seven braves running toward them inside the fort. Homer was surprised there were not more, making him wonder about the strength of the enemy. He fired his piece at the approaching Indians, and the others did the same. Three Indians crumpled to the ground.

"Come on, John!" screamed Church.

They plowed their way back to Winslow and the break in the palisade wall. Upon arriving, they could see that some of the men had made it over the log and were taking positions inside the palisade. Indians charged to meet them, and soon they were locked in hand-to-hand combat. Some of the struggles carried the combatants into the ditch where they hacked at each other with sword or tomahawk amid the tangled mass of dead bodies.

When Moseley saw Church and Homer arrive he sprang up, shouting, "The diversion worked! The men are through! Let's go!"

Winslow started to protest, but Moseley, Homer and Church had already started for the log.

Homer reached the log first. Halfway across, his foot slipped on the slush and blood, sending him careening into the ditch of bodies.

Some of the men in the ditch were still alive, and they grabbed at Homer's ankles, as he crawled toward the palisade. At the edge of the ditch he tried to climb out, but the spot was too steep and icy. A brave standing at the top of the wall spied him and sent an arrow down, landing within inches of his head.

He was panicking now, feeling like a trapped animal in a cage—knowing that sooner or later an arrow would find him. He looked back up at the log, hoping to see Church, but the snow made it impossible to see anything other than gray, misty figures charging across. He screamed for Church, but his voice joined with the shouts and wails of a hundred others.

Finally he saw that on the opposite side of the log, bodies were stacked so high they rose almost to ground level. He scrambled over, and using the bodies as a ladder he climbed out, then into the Indian fort.

Chapter 19

Napatoo lay terrified inside the wigwam, shuddering each time a musket boomed. She stayed close to a large bin of corn for protection against any stray musket balls, and she kept Chusett inside her beaverskin cloak. Her wigwam was one of the closest ones to the unfinished wall, no more than thirty yards from the opening.

As scared as she was, she was also filled with hate—hate for the whites that would attack a camp comprised primarily of women and children, and hate for Philip. Philip did this to us, she thought; we are not safe even in a swamp camp, even with the Narragansetts.

Suddenly the shouts of the soldiers and their accompanying musket fire were close by. Trembling, she crawled to the wigwam entrance and peered outside into the swirling snow. An old warrior was standing right next to the wigwam aiming his arrow toward the break in the palisade wall. She couldn't believe the warriors were falling back. The soldiers must be inside the camp!

Just then a musket ball hit the warrior square in the chest, spraying Napatoo's face with blood. She screamed in horror, the wind catching her cry and mingling it with all the others. She heard the dull thud of another ball hit the wigwam and a sack of corn. With a mother's instinct, she held Chusett tighter.

Time seemed to pass in slow motion. She prayed to the Great Creator for courage and direction. But a panic was rising inside her, a claustrophobic feeling of being trapped. She shut her eyes tightly and thought of Tamoset for comfort; she tried to see his face, smell his smell, feel his touch. "I love you," she whispered, hoping her spirit message would reach him.

The soldier's shouts were louder now. From nearby a woman shrieked. A terror filled her like she had never known, her heart raced, and she gasped for air. She couldn't stay there another minute, she couldn't let them come and kill her baby.

With Chusett wrapped firmly inside her cloak, she sprang up and dashed outside. A thick cloud of gunpowder mixed with the snow, making it impossible to see. She jumped over the dead warrior by the wigwam door, hearing a musket ball whiz past her ear. She dodged behind the next wigwam she saw, but another shot splintered the bark covering beside her. There was nowhere to hide. Her brain screamed, "Run! Run!" And she did.

She felt the ball plow into her back and lift her off her feet, sending her face first into the snow. "Tamoset," she cried. Then all was dark.

* * * *

Homer was badly shaken from his fall off the log. Inside the fort now, he crouched behind a dead soldier, using the corpse as protection from the arrows which seemed to come from all directions. He felt a hand on his shoulder, and spun to his side, frantically trying to reach for his knife.

"John! John! It's me," screamed Church. "Come on, I see Captain Gardner ahead."

Homer scrambled to his feet, dashing over to where Gardner was trying to organize the oncoming rush of soldiers that were pouring through the palisade opening.

Upon seeing Church, Gardner barked out orders, "I want the first fifty men to follow me around the left wall, and Church, you take ... ."

Gardner collapsed to ground.

Church knelt beside him and saw the blood running down his cheek. "Captain, hang on!" shouted Church just inches from his face.

But Gardner could only open his mouth, before the life passed from him.

Church removed the captain's hat and saw where the ball had entered his head. He immediately realized the shot had been fired from their rear—the Indians were behind them as well as in front.

A group of five soldiers gathered around the fallen captain. Church shouted above the commotion, "The devils are behind us! They must be in that corn crib! Let's go!"

Church led the way, and when he was within twenty feet of the corn crib the natives fired. Three shots hit him; the first passed through his pocket, the second nicked his stomach, and the third went into his thigh. He staggered, firing his piece wildly at the braves ahead.

Homer came running and wrapped an arm around him for support, leaving himself fully exposed. The natives saw the target and sent a fusillade of arrows at him; one hit the arm that held Church. Despite his wound, Homer managed to pull

Church away from the open ground to the back of a woodpile, where they collapsed.

They watched with satisfaction as their comrades took up positions around them and fired shot after shot into the corn crib. Soldiers were everywhere now, and the fort was in their control.

"Ben, there's Winslow!" said Homer, pointing through the swirling snow and gun powder.

"Notice how he enters after we've done all the dirty work," snapped Church through teeth clinched with pain. "We best get over there."

"You're wounded; stay down, I'll go get him."

"I'm all right, I'm more worried about my feet—I can't feel my toes; it feels like they're frozen. Besides, you're wounded yourself."

Homer looked at his bloodied left arm. He didn't dare take his coat off to inspect the wound. Then a blast of wind brought with it the strong smell of woodsmoke.

Church smelled it at the same instant.

"Fire! Can you see it, John?"

Homer peered around the edge of the woodpile and watched a wigwam go up in flames. Soldiers were running from wigwam to wigwam, pouring powder on each and then striking their flints. Suddenly a small Indian girl came dashing out of the first wigwam with hair on fire. Others were trapped inside, their screams carried on the wind.

"They're burning everything!" shouted Homer.

"Damn it! We need those wigwams—there's food inside, and we've got to get our wounded out of this snow. Help me up, John, I've got to stop that fool Winslow."

Church's pants were crimson with blood, as Homer half carried and half dragged him to where the Captain had positioned himself. Now the sky was filled with an eerie glow as sparks mixed with snow. Other wigwams were catching fire from the sparks, and visibility was no more than twenty feet through the thick smoke.

"Captain!" shouted Church, waving his arms. "Stop this madness!"

Winslow turned with surprise, "It's Church! He's hurt, someone get him to the rear."

"Never mind me; stop the burning! Listen to me, Captain. Those wigwams are full of corn, enough to supply us till spring. And we can put the wounded in there and ride out this storm. Hell, we'll loose half the troops going back to Wickford in this blizzard!"

Before Winslow could reply, one of his aides, the company's doctor, stepped up and addressed the Captain.

"Don't listen to him. We need to get the wounded moving before they stiffen up. We can't stay here. Burn every wigwam, I say! Let the Indians know our wrath. I don't care how many women and children go up in flames. Kill them now, so they don't breed in the spring!"

Church would have hit the Doctor, had not Homer been holding him. "Captain we can stay here and be protected by the palisade. It does us no good to kill women and children."

The doctor was furious, and he turned to Church pointing a long bony finger in his face, "You and your stinking advice, I'll let you bleed to death like a dog, before I attend your wounds."

Winslow puffed his chest, "Enough, enough of that!" He looked out at the smoke and fire. "Burn everything, and kill every Indian here. I'm not staying here through the night. We have no idea how many savages are nearby."

The orgy of death and fire went on until the entire camp was consumed. At dusk the soldiers grew anxious to leave, fearing that more natives would be coming like a swarm of angry bees to their broken hive. Order began to break down among the troops as rumors circulated that Canonchet and 2,000 warriors were on the way.

Finally, with darkness closing in, Winslow gave the instruction to form columns and march, leaving the village smouldering behind.

* * * *

The few Indians that had escaped from the camp inferno lay hidden nearby in the swamp. As soon as the troops were gone, the survivors re-entered the camp, hoping to save some provisions. They were horrified to see the charred remains of hundreds of women and children within the remains of the wigwams.

One young Narragansett boy went among the bodies of the dead warriors by the hole in the palisade, looking for any bits of food among them or a musket overlooked by the soldiers. After searching the area near the log entrance, the boy headed back toward where the other survivors had gathered.

On the way he stopped suddenly, hearing a whimper. It seemed to be coming from the lifeless form of a woman. He ran to the body, and rolled it over. She was clearly dead, and the boy was about to leave when he noticed a movement within her cloak. He opened it and was astonished to see a baby.

Chapter 20

He sat alone, staring out over frozen white hills. Napatoo and Chusett were dead. Tamoset repeated this over and over, forcing the reality inward.

Another bitter blast of wind roared over Wachusett Mountain, sweeping snow across the frozen landscape. His body shook, but he wasn't aware of the cold. So great was his heartache, it used up his entire capacity for pain.

He kept his eyes on the southern horizon, seeing nothing yet seeing all. Snatches of memories of Napatoo played across his mind: her smile, her touch, her slender frame. And there was Chusett, with the big, sparkling eyes of wonder. Each vision intensified the pain, but there was no stopping them.

Two days ago the world as Tamoset knew it had ended. Word had come that the Narragansett camp had been wiped out. All women and children were killed, most were burned alive in their wigwams.

Upon hearing this, Tamoset walked out of the Wachusett camp in a dazed stupor. For the past two days he had wandered around the rugged hills, not eating or sleeping, blaming himself for the deaths of his wife and child. He should have been there, he told himself over and over, should have been protecting them. He had promised Napatoo he would return; he had promised they would be safe.

He thought how Napatoo had begged him not to follow Philip, how she had appealed to his responsibility as a father. If only he had listened, he would still have her by his side, still have Chusett bouncing on his knee. They were the only ones that mattered.

Instead, he was utterly alone, not caring if he lived or died. Philip had persuaded him that the tribe needed him more. And now where was the tribe? Some had been killed at the Narragansett camp; the rest were scattered in all directions, their homeland in the hands of the whites.

Tamoset endured this dark night of the soul, depression giving way to anger. He hated himself, he hated Philip, but he hated the English more. They were the ones that would pay. They would suffer for taking his world away.

He spent one more miserable night alone in the woods. At dawn he walked back to camp, going directly to Philip's wigwam.

Philip was alone, wrapped in a wolf cape, smoking beside a small fire. He looked up at Tamoset, and without saying a word, handed him the pipe. Tamoset took the pipe and sat opposite the fire, both men looking into the flames.

Philip could feel his friend's grief but there was nothing he could say of comfort. His own wife and child were safe with the Nipmucks back at the Connecticut River camp, but as Sachem, Philip suffered too; half his tribe was dead.

Tamoset broke the silence, "Tomorrow we start on the warpath. We will attack many towns."

It was not a question, not a request, but a statement. With or without Philip, Tamoset would raid English towns.

Philip looked up from the fire and gave a slight nod. He had been planning the same thing. He needed a victory. His people had made no significant attacks since leaving the Connecticut River.

As if talking to himself, Philip mused, "If only we can get the Mohawks to join us ... ." He put another stick on the fire, then looked into his friend's eyes. For the first time he noticed how awful Tamoset looked. His face was thin from lack of food, and the scar was an ugly purplish color from the extreme cold.

Philip continued, "I'll talk to more tribes while you lead the attacks. Raid at sunrise when the English are at their weakest. Hit Lancaster first, and then move southeastward toward Boston and Dedham."

Tamoset stood, passing the pipe back to Philip. "I'll tell the others." Then he went out into the snow.

Chapter 21

John Homer lay in bed, his eyes open in the darkness. Elizabeth was sleeping beside him.

Another nightmare of the massacre at the Great Swamp had awakened Homer. This time the dream was of a native girl running with her hair in flames. The dream was horrifying, but no more than what Homer had seen in the actual attack.

He slowly got out of bed and tip-toe'd over to the common room, where the fire in the massive hearth had died down to glowing embers. The small house was freezing. He lit a candle, then placed three new logs on the coals.

Sleep seemed impossible, so he fished in the back of the cupboard for a hidden jug of rum and poured himself half a mug.

"John, what is it?"

Homer spun around, surprised to see Elizabeth.

"I'm fine, go back to bed," he said gruffly.

Elizabeth walked over to the long pine table and sat down on the bench.

"Sit down, John. Won't you talk to me?"

Homer took a sip of rum and joined her at the table.

"It was awful," he said with a sigh. "The whole bloody thing was awful."

She reached out and lay her hand on his. "Time will help, John, time and the Lord."

"Don't talk to me about the Lord," he snapped, "right now its hard to believe there's a God."

Elizabeth winced, but said nothing.

The rum was spreading through him, warming him like the sun. He looked at his mug, and continued in a softer voice, "Such carnage. Bodies filled the ditch. Inside the camp it was like hell—screaming, smoke and this sickening smell of burning flesh. At the time I barely noticed it, too busy running, dodging arrows and musket balls. But now I can't stop thinking about it."

Elizabeth encouraged him to talk more, but he shook his head. She tried changing the subject. "Maybe its time we send the children to Boston."

"Yes," he nodded looking up at her. "The news from Lancaster came as a terrible surprise, but it could happen here."

Lancaster had just been attacked, scores were dead, and others had been carried off alive to an unknown fate, probably torture and death.

A cold chill raised goosebumps on Elizabeth's back. The very word Lancaster caused her instant fear. "Surely, the Governor will send us more troops," she said shakily.

"Not probable, he already responded to our letter."

Homer was referring to the eighty troops that had arrived a few days earlier.

The citizens of Medfield had written Governor Leverett describing their town as a "frontier town" ripe for attack by the "cannibals." They tried to convince the Governor that they were strategic to Boston's safety: "The loss of Medfield will be a very great blow: what will become of the city if the hands of the country grow feeble?"

Medfield had hoped for at least 200 soldiers, but Leverett was getting similar pleas from towns throughout the Massachusetts Bay Colony. People were terrified, and some towns were totally defenseless.

Homer stood up, noticing the first hint of gray dawn through the room's tiny window. "I'm going to start chores early."

He put on pants, shirt, coat and hat, then he lifted the door latch and made his way toward the barn. Snow crunched underfoot. As he walked, shoulders hunched against the cold, he decided to send Elizabeth to Boston with the children. Even if the town stays safe, he thought, no sense subjecting her to my sleepless nights and foul mood.

In the barn, the cattle stood quietly, steam rising from their nostrils. The cold had them in a kind of frozen stupor. Homer grabbed a pitchfork and started shoveling hay into the stalls.

On his third stab at the hay his eyes widened—a moccasin was sticking out of the pile he was working on. Above the moccasin he could see the vague outline of a leg. A native was hiding in the hay!

For a split second he considered spearing the Indian with his pitchfork. Instead, he went to work on a different part of the pile, pretending not to have seen a thing. With arms trembling and heartbeat hammering in his head, he continued throwing hay.

His mind raced through a series questions: How many could there be? Should I run and get my musket? Should I run to the neighbors? He thought of Elizabeth and the children. Got to get them to safety before I do anything.

He quietly placed the pitchfork against the nearest stall and forced himself to walk at a normal pace back to the house. Inside, he grabbed Elizabeth. "Wake the children," he hissed. "then follow me. Indians. Don't say a word."

He then took his musket off the pegs above the fireplace, quickly pouring powder in the pan and ramming a ball down the shaft.

Within seconds Elizabeth had the children up. She kept a shaking finger to her lips in the sign of silence.

"We go out the back door," whispered Homer. "Stay close to me, no one talks."

"But father—"

Homer shot Jeremiah a dark glance and the boy went mute.

Out they went, still in their nightshirts. The house shielded them from the barn, and Homer prayed they had not been seen. They broke into a run, heading toward the center of town.

When Homer could see the garrison in the distance, he shouted for Elizabeth to take the kids without him. She stopped to protest, but he waved her on as he started back toward the farm. He glanced once over his shoulder and saw them safely enter.

Upon reaching the crest of the hill at the outskirts of town, his heart stopped. Thirty warriors were charging up the road, coming directly at him. Behind them smoke was pouring from his barn and house.

He leveled his musket at the braves and fired. Then he spun around, sprinting back toward the garrison. Ahead, he could see other families doing the same—they had heard the musket shot and wasted no time running for the safety of the garrison.

The freezing February air stung his lungs. He glanced back and saw that two of the braves were gaining on him. A musket ball whizzed past his ear. Adrenaline coursed through his body and his legs pumped faster.

He looked back again. One warrior was only ten yards away. Something about the warrior looked vaguely familiar. He was short and thickly muscled, but he ran like the wind, gaining on Homer with every step.

Homer expected to be slammed by a musket ball at any second. He dropped his heavy musket and ran with every ounce of strength. Once he came within view of the garrison the soldiers inside saw his predicament, and fired a barrage at the pack chasing him. Three braves dropped, but the lead man and the others veered off the road and took cover behind nearby buildings and trees.

Once at the garrison doorway, Homer dove through, tumbling to the floor. The soldiers shut and bolted the door behind him—more natives were converging on the garrison from all directions.

From the musket holes, soldiers could see that other settlers were still outside, running toward the garrison. But one by one they were caught and tomahawked by the swifter braves. One settler was beheaded on the spot, his head then tossed like a ball from warrior to warrior.

Homer staggered to his feet, was given a musket, and stationed himself at a shooting hole. Musket balls rattled against the fort like hail. He watched as braves went inside a barn and emerged with burning hay.

"Shoot those with the fire first!" he screamed. "If the garrison catches fire that's the end of us!"

Recklessly, the natives charged. Again Homer saw the short warrior who had almost caught him. Now he could see that his face was scarred, and knew it was the very same one he had shot at the first swamp battle. He took aim and fired.

Tamoset zig-zagged. The musket ball missed him by an inch. He continued running like a man possessed, his only thought to kill everyone inside. Now he was at the side of the garrison. Someone inside shot through the wall but the musket ball went wide of Tamoset. He threw his torch on the roof, then ran back to the barn.

Inside the garrison, chaos reigned. Blood covered the floor where a half dozen people lay dead. Others were wounded and crying from pain.

A women screamed, "Lord, what shall we do?"

"God tests us!" bellowed the Reverend.

A second later a musket ball smashed into his head, sending his brains spattering all over the hysterical woman.

Homer's eyes watered from all the musket smoke. As he reloaded, he wondered about the scar-faced Indian—he was sure he had killed him at the swamp. But he was quite alive; in fact, he was the one who had put the torch to his home and barn—twenty years of work gone up in smoke. He prayed Elizabeth and the children were safe on the second floor above.

"Fire, fire!" shouted a soldier scrambling down the stairs. "Get the buckets!"

While some grabbed buckets that had been kept full for such an emergency, Homer grabbed an axe and ran upstairs. Women and children cowered in a corner, coughing from the thick smoke that filled the room. Flames were already visible on the inside of the roof threatening to engulf the entire structure.

With swinging axe, Homer attacked the wood that was on fire. "Get over here with blankets!" he roared to a nearby woman. "Smother the flaming wood that falls!"

He hacked a large hole in the roof. Blue sky could be seen above. He pushed a small bureau underneath the hole. Soldiers arrived with buckets, and Homer grabbed the first one. He stood on top of the bureau and stuck the bucket through the opening to have the water hit the flames from the outside.

A soldier got on the bureau next to him and followed his lead. "More water!" commanded the young soldier to those below. Another bucket was handed to him, and he stuck his head out the hole again.

He glanced at Homer, "It's working, we did—ahhhggg."

His voice turned into a gasping, slurping noise, and his hands went to his throat. An arrow was sticking out of his neck. Blood was spurting from the front of the wound. Homer reached over and grabbed his collar, but the man collapsed and went crashing below.

Arrows were landing all around Homer, and he ducked back inside. "One more bucket, quick!"

He put the bucket back up through the hole and an arrow bounced off it, saving Homer's life in the process. He splashed the water on the last of the flames.

Elizabeth shrieked below. "John! John! Daniel's been hit! God, please no!"

Homer's youngest son, Daniel, had stood by the bureau to watch his father when a musket ball blasted through a chink in the garrison wall and hit him in the chest.

Homer raced to where Elizabeth cradled the boy. He knelt beside them and stroked the hair of the unconscious boy. Just then a tremendous boom filled the air, shaking the building. The soldiers shouted, "The cannon, the other garrison fired the cannon! They will hear it in Dedham! Help is on the way!"

And then from downstairs a wild whoop filled the house. "The demons are pulling back! Praise God, we made it!"

Homer paid no attention; Daniel had stopped breathing.

Chapter 22

The war party pulled back toward the Charles River, setting fire to every building along the way. Sheep, horses and cattle were either killed or taken away for food. A handful of captives, pulled by a rope around their necks, staggered behind the warriors.

Tamoset saw a brave rush into a burning building and emerge with an armful of clothing. "Leave it," shouted Tamoset, "take only their animals!"

The warrior, a Narragansett, was not used to taking orders from a Wampanoag. He continued walking with his arms loaded. "I do as I like," he snarled.

Tamoset was in no mood to argue; he was leading this raid, and he would not be challenged. Pulling his tomahawk from his belt, he walked straight at the Narragansett.

Seeing the look in Tamoset's eyes, the warrior thought better of his decision and dropped the plunder.

Tamoset turned to the others, "I'll kill the next man that challenges me."

The men stood silently.

Tamoset pointed down the road to the bridge crossing the river. "We go now. Burn the bridge behind us, then you can celebrate all you want."

Once across the river, a huge fire was built, and the triumphant warriors roasted an ox. Tamoset sat apart from the group, looking back across the river at the smoke still rising from Medfield. Occasionally a brave came up and congratulated him on the victory.

A warrior named James-the-Printer wandered over and struck up a conversation with Tamoset. Before taking to the warpath, James had lived at the Praying Indian community of Natick, and he could both speak and write English. The two men had talked before—Tamoset wanted to learn all he could about the enemy that killed his family.

"Tamoset, you led us to a great victory. We have taken many scalps and have five captives."

"Yes, we hurt them badly, most of the town is in ashes. The English are fools, they do not fire the woods in the spring, and the brush made it easy for us to sneak up on the town."

"Where will we go next?"

"Does it matter? Just as long as we drive the strangers toward the sea. They still are farming in towns like Sudbury, Marlboro and Groton. We must wipe out the farms so they have no food. We must hit and run. Along the Connecticut we stayed too long trying to burn their safe-houses—we lost too many braves."

James clasped Tamoset on the shoulder. "Soon we will burn Boston itself!" he said, turning to walk back to the celebration.

"Wait," said Tamoset. "I want you to write a message to the English."

* * * *

After the warriors had feasted on the ox, Tamoset led them northward to strike again. Tacked to the remains of the bridge he left behind a note:

"Know by this paper, that the Indians that thou hast provoked to wrath and anger, will war this twenty-one years if you will: there are many Indians yet, we come three hundred this time. You must consider the Indians lost nothing but their life; you must lose your fair houses and cattle."

Chapter 23

Winter's icy grip had a firm hold during February. The Wachusett camp swelled in size with a steady stream of Narragansetts. Most arrived with little more than tattered moccasins and worn-out capes. More people meant less food to go around, and all suffered the ache of hunger.

Quinna sat with a group of women in a wigwam, sewing. Each day they worked together performing a variety of critical tasks; shelling groundnuts, preparing furs for clothing, or making mats for the wigwams. Today they were sewing moccasins.

They talked as they worked, much of the conversation centering on a common homesickness. With spring approaching, they wondered if they would return to tribal lands for the growing season and the fish runs. One woman blamed all their misery on Philip. Quinna didn't see it that way, but she held her tongue. It wasn't worth the effort to argue.

Seated alone in the darkness at the rear of the wigwam was a captive, Mary Rowlandson. The warmth of the fire hardly reached her there, and her fingers shook as she read her bible. She had been captured in Lancaster two weeks earlier. Through sheer determination and a will to live, she had survived when other captives were clubbed on the head as soon as they became a burden.

But now she thought her very blood would freeze from the cold, and she decided to risk edging closer to the fire.

One of the older woman seated at the fire was her master. "Ho," said the old Indian. "You think you have earned a place by the fire?"

"I'll freeze to death back there!" came Rowlandson's angry response in English.

"Maybe you will find it more comfortable outside," said her mistress sarcastically. "Your book will keep you warm. Now get out, before we put you closer to the fire than you'd like!"

When Rowlandson didn't move fast enough, the old woman yanked a stick from the fire and struck her on the back. Sparks shot to and fro, as Rowlandson scrambled toward the wigwam opening, knowing that her mistress could have her killed at any second.

Quinna got up and followed the white woman out. "Follow me," she said, leading her toward the wigwam she shared with Ochala.

Both women suddenly stopped walking, and they turned their heads toward the south. Far in the distance they heard a dull din, growing louder with each passing second. Soon they recognized the sounds as shouts from people whooping and roaring. Quinna knew it was warriors returning, their shouts signifying a victory.

Now the whole village could hear the approaching thunder, and everyone dashed from the wigwams to welcome the braves. For a moment Quinna and Rowlandson forgot the cold, spellbound by this oncoming roar.

A mighty cheer went up when the braves burst upon the village, running straight toward Philip's wigwam. Quinna recognized Tamoset as the lead warrior by his short and powerful frame. She watched him coming toward her. Closer now, she could see his face. Thin and gaunt, his mouth was set in a tight line. Gone was the thoughtful look she had come to know him by. He looked neither to the right nor left, but led his warriors straight ahead. He passed so close to Quinna she could have touched him. She tried to make eye contact, but he only stared ahead as if he were the only person for miles around.

He was past her now, and Quinna involuntarily shuddered. She could see he had changed, could see he was in a world of his own, acrid and unapproachable.

A deep melancholy swept over her. She knew Tamoset had lost both wife and child in the Great Swamp. She barely knew the man, but her heart ached for his pain. He had been different than the others, but now he seemed to be a wild animal, wounded and dangerous. Any chance at getting to know him better seemed lost.

More warriors were running by, some with scalps waving from their belts, others holding sheep or pigs. Then the injured warriors came. One quick look told Quinna that most would not survive the night. They were carried by healthy braves, but still their blood dripped, leaving a trail of crimson on the snow. For the past twenty-four hours they had doggedly clung to life, trying to hang on just long enough to make the triumphant entrance back to their people. Then they would give up their lives. It was important that the whole village see their self-sacrifice.

After the wounded came the captives. They were not bound. They knew that to try to escape meant instant death. Besides, there was nowhere to go in this vast forest. They would not survive one night in the bitter cold. No, they could only hope that they would eventually be ransomed.

Word quickly spread that the warriors were coming from Medfield where they had destroyed the town. Most of the villagers followed the warriors toward Philip's wigwam to begin the celebration. But Quinna wanted to be alone. Seeing Tamoset, seeing the dying braves, and seeing the miserable captives was enough. When will it stop? she wondered.

She motioned for Rowlandson to follow her, and they walked away from the crowd to her wigwam, where she knew Ochala would be waiting.

Chapter 24

The granite ledge was situated in such a way that it blocked the breeze but captured what little warmth there was from the sun. Tamoset sat there, staring down at the ground where he had positioned small stones in an arc around a larger stone. The big stone represented Boston, and the smaller ones were the surrounding towns such as Groton, Chelmsford and Marlborough to the north and west, and Plymouth and Weymouth to the south.

The thought of the next attack consumed him. He knew his braves needed three or four days of food and rest before starting out again, but Tamoset was ready now, just one day after his return to the Wachusett camp. He had spent all morning listening to the reports of scouts. He learned which towns were unprotected, where the English forces were concentrated and more.

He was becoming knowledgeable in the ways of war; to understand your enemy is the key to victory. Attacking well-fortified towns and garrisons was wasting braves; Tamoset preferred to hit the isolated towns first, slowly tightening the noose around Boston. And if small bands of English soldiers were foolish enough to venture into the forest, he would lie in wait.

The war which had ruined his life, now gave him a reason to live. Revenge brought a perverse kind of satisfaction. The destruction of Medfield had been complete—he couldn't wait to do it to another town. He thought of Medfield.

Something about the Englishman he chased to the garrison haunted him. Tall and thin, he fought well, too. Could it be the same man at the first swamp fight, the one who gave me this scar? he asked himself. Maybe. But I hate him no more than the rest. We burned his farm. He loves the land as I do. But only one people can live here. This is a war to the end.

"Tamoset."

He looked up and saw the towering figure of Philip. Philip sat down next to him, picked up a rock and placed it far to the south of the Boston stone.

"We must not forget Roger William's Town," said Philip, referring to Providence.

"Yes," nodded Tamoset, "we will destroy that, too."

"Do so with Canonchet; he will be eager for revenge."

Tamoset winced, thinking of the Great Swamp massacre. The pain would not leave him; it was always close to the surface.

Philip saw the cloud pass over his friend's face and averted his eyes, wishing to comfort him but not knowing how. They were close, like brothers, and like many brothers most feelings went unsaid.

"You led us to great victory at Medfield."

"Yes," Tamoset agreed, eyes distant, mind still on Napatoo and Chusett. "We burned most of their farms."

"That is good. The English worship their farms, their tools, their possessions. They have no spirit lives; that is why they are soft, that is why they are cowards."

Tamoset knew this was true. As he faced Philip for the first time, he thought how much his friend seemed to have aged. New lines had creased his face, his skin was taut against high cheekbones and a prominent nose. But his eyes still had the fire, and he still looked much the part of the leader. Feathers from a hawk fanned out from the back of his skull. And although he was thinner, he still seemed to have that cat-like power just beneath the surface.

"One thing I learned at Medfield," said Tamoset, still looking at Philip, "is that we lose many braves at the garrisons. We should leave the English to their garrisons, and while they hide like women, we can burn the town, losing fewer braves."

Philip spat on the ground, then shook his head from side to side. "Kill them all, I say. Don't let them live to fight another day."

Tamoset knew it was futile to discuss the subject further. Philip's pride simply would not let him see the logic in avoiding the garrisons.

Philip rose to his feet.

"Let us get something to eat. One of the braves has killed a deer; finally some meat."

When Tamoset rose, Philip gripped him by the arm.

"Tamoset, when you attack the next town, let the other braves go first. You are a leader. I can't afford to lose you."

Their eyes met for a second.

"I understand," said Tamoset, acknowledging but not committing to Philip's request.

Philip released the arm. There was nothing more to say. Together they left the rock ledge and walked back toward the center of the camp.

* * * *

Quinna carried a large wooden bowl toward the stream. Mary Rowlandson followed behind, her dress torn and soiled, her hair matted and snarled. She hacked a terrible cough, and hunger pains racked her stomach. Yet she knew better than to voice her misery. She had seen what happened to captives who complained.

A pregnant white woman, who had a young child with her, begged for food constantly. Finally her master had heard enough: the captive was taken outside the wigwam and stripped. A crowd gathered, hurling insults. In due time, her master slammed a tomahawk into the back of her head, killing her instantly. Then he grabbed the child by its feet and slammed its head against a tree trunk.

Rowlandson had been through hell. Her own baby had died in her arms from exposure just three days after being taken. She had other children who she knew had also been taken captive, but had no idea of their whereabouts. At times she felt herself slip into a stupor of depression and anguish, but somehow her will to survive carried her, just as it did now, helping Quinna to get water. She knew that to stay alive she must be useful; her captors barely had enough food for themselves.

Rowlandson was free to walk around the camp. Her mistress made it clear that if caught escaping she would be tortured. Besides, she would not survive one winter night in the woods—woods where wolves howled each night, lurking just beyond the edge of the camp. Her mistress told her they would be leaving soon, probably going westward to the Great River. Until then Rowlandson had to fend for herself.

Since the preceding afternoon, when Quinna showed her kindness, she had stayed close to the young Indian woman, helping her in any way possible. Some of the Indians knew a little English, but Quinna spoke none, so they did not communicate except through gestures. Still, Rowlandson had already grown to admire Quinna's stoicism and resourcefulness. She could tell this was a woman of courage, independence and compassion by the way she looked after her old father.

As they approached the stream, Rowlandson saw two braves coming from the other direction. She immediately recognized one as Philip—he knew some English and had already spoken to her once before. The other man had a grotesque purple scar across his face.

Quinna signaled a greeting when the men were closer.

Philip went straight to Rowlandson and stared at the small woman. Before the war he had known a couple of English families near Montaup. He and the men would talk of hunting, and in the early years they would inquire about his father, Massasoit.

In broken English Philip said, "I have tobacco for you."

Rowlandson hesitated a moment, surprised at the sachem's offer. "Thank you."

Philip nodded. "Come by my wigwam later; we have a little deer meat and corn cakes, too."

Rowlandson's mouth watered at the very words, and her shrunken stomach sent out a sharp pain. Her mind worked quickly.

"Thank you, I will make you a shirt and bring it with me."

"No," said Philip, "make cap for my son; someday soon I see him."

Rowlandson agreed, gave a slight bow of her head and, taking the bowl from Quinna, went on to get the water.

Quinna stood watching the exchange, not knowing the English words, nevertheless astonished by the friendly tone. Tamoset, however, was not surprised. Nothing his friend did surprised him anymore. Philip was a complex man, capable of many moods, often going out of his way to show kindness to those less fortunate.

Tamoset looked at Quinna. She looked as beautiful as the day he first saw her. He had not talked to her since their last exchange at the camp by the Great River. Recalling the night he kissed her, mistaking friendship for something more, he shifted uncomfortably. He would never touch rum again. A sense of guilt spread over him; he would rather not see her again.

Finally, he found his voice.

"How is Ochala?" he asked, a nuetral subject, someone they both cared for.

"He is feeling his age, perhaps it is the cold."

Tamoset decided to see the old man soon. Ochala reminded him of his own father, a man of few words but much wisdom.

Philip broke in, smiling down on Quinna.

"Ochala is a wise man. His counsel is important to me; he talks from the heart. You are fortunate to have such a man for a father."

"Yes. Ochala thinks maybe now we will win the struggle. He thinks the Great Creator is on our side, that this bad winter makes the English afraid to take to the field."

Tamoset thought to himself: Already she has forgotten the English march on the Great Swamp. The weather did not stop them then.

Philip cocked his head.

"When cautious Ochala thinks we will win, I know it for certain. Tell him that come planting season we will be in Boston itself." Then, turning to Tamoset, he said, "Come, let us go to my wigwam and plan the next attack."

The men walked off. Quinna stood alone for a moment. She had wanted to talk to Tamoset but now was not the time. He hates me, she thought; he is not the same man as before.

She turned toward the stream, thinking: I'll never have his friendship, never be able to tell him about the dreams I keep having about his son. Strange dreams, but real, maybe more real than today. I know he is not ready to talk; the wound is open, may always be open.

She sighed, wondering if she would ever meet the right man, then followed the icy path to the stream where Rowlandson was waiting.

Chapter 25

"Do you trust them?" Homer whispered, eyes glued to the trail ahead.

"Don't think we have a choice," said George Oliver, Homer's marching companion.

Up ahead two Christian natives, armed with muskets, warily scouted the woodland trail. A thick stand of hemlocks stood on the right, and on the left was a swamp, still frozen on this late March afternoon. By now Homer and the rest of the men knew the makings of an ambush.

Dusk was coming on, and the trees cast long shadows on the frozen ground. The scouts had reached the center of the trail, the point where most ambushes were sprung. Homer held his breath. He was lying in the snow, shaking from cold, musket loaded and pointed straight ahead. Any minute he expected to hear a war whoop.

The scouts made it to the end of the narrow passage. Now each would double back, reconnoitering farther off the trail for signs of the enemy. One went into the swamp, and the other disappeared in the hemlocks.

Oliver blew on his frozen fingers, "This is the worst part. The waiting."

Homer nodded. Four minutes went by. Occasionally they could hear a faint tinkling noise from the scout in the frozen swamp. The ice was like glass crystals, and even the scout's superior stealth could not keep them completely silent.

"What's taking them so long? They should be back by now," hissed Homer anxiously through dry, cracked lips. He was exhausted from three days of marching westward toward the Connecticut River and the garrison at Hadley. Homer and the other volunteers made the trip at great peril, moving as quickly and quietly as possible through over sixty miles of virgin forest controlled by hostile natives. So far they had been lucky and encountered none. But now Homer was on edge, expecting the worse.

"Easy, John. It's only been a few minutes. These scouts have brought us this far safely, let them do their work." Oliver's words were meant to soothe, but he, too, expected the woods to erupt at any moment. He kept looking toward the hemlocks, thinking that if there is an ambush, that's where the Indians will be hiding.

Another couple of minutes went by; then the two scouts emerged from the brush. They motioned for the soldiers to follow.

Oliver stood first, shaking the snow off. "I hate having my life in their hands, but if we had come without them, our hair would probably be hanging from the top of some wigwam."

Homer agreed. He, too, was uncomfortable with the scouts, yet if they meant harm it would probably have occurred by now. He was amazed at how the scouts could read the trail, telling them how long ago a party of braves had passed, where to find frozen groundnuts for food, and even predicting the snow that had fallen the previous night. But still they were natives, and since the death of his son, he hated all of them with a passion, even these two allies.

The twenty soldiers, all volunteers from Medfield and Dedham, were on their feet again, following the scouts to the west. They were on their way toward a secret mission on the western frontier. Although they had no idea what or when they would strike, they knew that they would be under the command of Captain Turner.

At first, Homer was upset that they should be assigned to a garrison so far from home, especially when there was trouble enough in the eastern part of the Bay Colony. But, when he learned they would be joining Turner, he was eager to go. Maybe now, he thought, we will locate Philip.

Turner might even turn the tables and lay an ambush or two for the natives. Like Benjamin Church, he had the reputation for bold action that went beyond merely guarding a town. He was not afraid to take to the woods and meet the enemy on their own turf.

The war had hardened Homer. He no longer had any remorse about the killing he had done, no longer thought about how the natives had been cheated from their land. He had never seen Philip, had no idea what he even looked like, but he had a personal hatred for the man that had started this. Now, when Homer dreamed, it was not of the horrors of war, but rather of seeing Philip, the mighty "King Philip," and blowing his head off with a musket ball.

They marched on, camping for the night in a pine grove. The scouts said that tomorrow morning they would be at the river. Oliver and Homer spread their blankets on pine boughs.

Half the men would sleep first while the other half served as sentries, then they would rotate. No fires were allowed.

"How's the feet, John?" asked Oliver, settling in under his blankets. He had noticed his friend limping throughout the day.

"Still there, I reckon, but not like they used to be. Ever since the Great Swamp they haven't been the same. Frostbite, hurts like hell." Homer liked Oliver. He was a grizzled blacksmith from Dedham, but he had the knack for soldiering and was tough as the anvil he worked over.

"Well, at least you didn't waste your energies that time. You boys got 'em good down in the swamp. Was mighty glad to hear you killed the squaws and all the rest. Keep em from breeding new ones."

Homer felt a spasm of anguish rush through him. Oliver had unwittingly reminded him of the death of his own son. The boy was only four years old when he was killed during the Medfield raid, and Homer felt like he hardly knew him. Between working in the fields from sunup to sundown and then the war, he rarely saw the little fellow. Now he would never see him again.

Oliver wondered why his friend stopped talking. Must be worn out, he thought. We both best get some rest. Our shift will be up in four hours. He settled down in the pine boughs looking up at a thousand stars above. Maybe we aren't meant for this cursed land, he thought, maybe the Lord is trying to tell us to get out. He shivered, closed his eyes and wondered if spring would ever come.

Chapter 26

Tamoset pulled hard on the paddle to keep pace with his companion, and the canoe glided downstream rapidly. Ice extended out from each bank like frozen fingers groping for something solid. In the center of the river, however, the water, black as night, was moving.

Temperatures had moderated, and Tamoset was glad to be off the trail, using his arms rather than legs. He could feel the power of the large man at the stern of the dugout canoe because with every stroke the canoe shot forward. Not once during the day had his companion rested, just one stroke after the other, each a long, fluid motion.

The man in the rear was Canonchet, the great Narragansett sachem. He was an imposing figure; a full six feet tall. His hair was streaked with gray, but his bare arms showed muscles even larger than Tamoset's.

"We've covered many miles. Soon we'll rest. Roger William's Town is not far now," said Canonchet in his deep, distinctive voice.

Tamoset turned his head to the side, "It is good to be on the water again."

"You have traveled far and often. This journey will be another victory, friend."

Tamoset thought back over the last few months. Since leaving Montaup, he had covered hundreds of miles, leaving a path of destruction in his wake. Just a few days ago he made a raid on a garrison at Plymouth, killing eighteen English. Then they traveled west raiding more towns; Taunton and Rehoboth were hit especially hard. Now they were moving south through Narragansett country toward the Quaker's Rhode Island.

He thought of the last time he was in the region, the day before the war started, the day he tried to persuade Canonchet to join Philip. So long ago, he thought; I had much to learn. He remembered swimming in the pond with Ponotuck on the outskirts of the Narragansett village. Ponotuck's dead now; was he really a traitor? Tamoset could only wonder.

And he thought of Napatoo, always saw her face, always felt the guilt. If only he had acted on the vision. He thought back; I knew the river running red was our people's blood; I could have taken Napatoo far away from here. Revenge was the only thing that numbed the pain.

As if reading his thoughts, the voice from behind said softly, "I should have listened to you the first time we met." He paused, gave two mighty pulls on the paddle, and went on, "Now your wife and child are gone and so are many of my people."

Tamoset was surprised by Canonchet's honesty: it was rare for a leader to admit he was wrong. He did not answer. There was nothing to say. He knew that Canonchet had lost one of his own wives in the Great Swamp massacre, knew that he had the same pain. Revenge united the two men. Now the English would pay again. Providence would be burned, and woe to the settler caught outside the garrison!

When Tamoset didn't answer, Canonchet continued, "We will talk to Roger Williams before we destroy his town. I will give him the chance to leave. I will tell him why we do this. I owe him that much."

Tamoset kept his eyes on the river ahead. A flock of red-winged blackbirds chirped noisily from their tree roosts. He didn't think Canonchet owed Roger Williams anything, except a hatchet through the skull. Had not Roger Williams let the soldiers from Massachusetts and Plymouth march through his colony to make the cowardly attack on the Great Swamp?

They continued downstream, silently passing by hundreds of muskrat lodges that stood frozen along the adjacent marshland. When the sun peeked from behind a cloud, the landscape was so bright, so white from the snow and ice, that it hurt the eyes. But Tamoset welcomed the sun. Today was the first day above the freezing mark in over two months.

Two hours later they pulled out at a great rock, just two miles above Providence. A messenger was sent for Roger Williams. Scouts were posted all around the meeting place in case the English tried a surprise attack.

While Tamoset and Canonchet waited, more braves arrived at the camp. Many of the lesser sachems wanted to attack immediately, but Canonchet would hear none of it. There was no rush; most of the citizens of Providence had fled days earlier.

Tamoset could hear the horses long before he could see them. Roger Williams and his aids had arrived. A hush fell over the camp, and Canonchet stood to greet his old friend.

Williams needed help getting from his horse; the portly old man had been ill, and worry over the war had taken its toll. He knew the Indians had come to burn the town he had built, knew that it was dangerous to come unarmed among the Indians. But Canonchet said he would be safe, and Canonchet had always kept his word. Maybe, just maybe, he will listen to reason, thought Williams.

"I am glad you remembered me, Canonchet," said Williams, hobbling to the campfire with the aid of a cane.

"You know why I am here," Canonchet said bluntly.

Williams nodded, then said, "Surely you will listen to the words of an old friend."

"I will listen. But I called you here out of respect. And I called you here to take a message to the English in Plymouth. Tell them I give warning before I attack, like a true warrior."

Then, glancing at Tamoset, he added, "Tell them I will be coming with the Wampanoags and Nipmucks to Plymouth and then to Boston."

"Canonchet, I know the hatred in your breast, but you cannot hope to win. The colonies can raise thousands of men, and old England can send more. Let us talk of peace. We lived together for many years; do not follow the foolish ways of Philip."

Tamoset stared at Williams. The word "Philip" was the first he understood, but he knew that Williams was talking of peace. He hated the fat Englishman; how could he talk of peace when he had allowed the massacre of women and children at the Great Swamp?

Tamoset listened closely, gauging the mood of the conversation. He was relieved to see Canonchet shaking his head no.

The old sachem's mind was made up; he would burn Providence. This meeting was his way of saying goodbye to Williams.

After more fruitless talk, Williams stood up. He shocked Tamoset by switching from English to the native dialect.

"Good bye, Canonchet. You are a noble man, but you are wrong."

"Go now. Once we could have talked, made council, but now it is too late."

Williams rode off, head down, wondering how things could have gotten so out of hand.

Canonchet turned to Tamoset. "We will burn the town. Leave nothing standing except Roger William's house. After we are done, return to Philip. Tell him I will join him in a few days, then together we will strike Boston."

Chapter 27

"No! You are wrong. He can't be dead!" Philip shook his head from side to side as if to throw off such a thought.

Tamoset kept his gaze on his friend and repeated, "Canonchet is dead."

Philip closed his eyes, suddenly tired and weary to the bone. In the background he could hear braves celebrating. They have no idea how bad this is, he thought, listening to the pounding of the drums. He opened his eyes, started to speak, then stopped. A slow anger was rising, and he waited for control to return. I must not blame Tamoset, he said to himself; it's not his fault.

Tamoset tipped his head back, looked at the sky and let out a long sigh. "This is what happened. We attacked Providence. It was easy; the people had already run like dogs. We burned almost every square house. Only one brave was killed. When it was over I saw Canonchet again. He was quiet but seemed pleased with the raid, telling me again that he would come here to Wachusett in just a few days. I said that—"

"You should have stopped him!" Philip barked.

An uneasy silence followed. Tamoset stared at Philip, but ignored his comment and continued.

"Three days later word came that Canonchet had been captured. English soldiers from Connecticut, aided by many Mohegans, surprised him."

Philip exploded. "Traitors! The Mohegans again! We will kill every one of them!" His lips were pinched tight and his chest heaved. The magnitude of losing such an ally was almost more than he could bear.

Tamoset waited for the rage to pass. When Philip said no more, he finished his story.

"They took him to Connecticut and killed him. There was nothing we could do. We did not know he was captured until three days later. Some of his braves came with me here, but most are still fighting to the south."

Philip stood, shaking with anger, drew his hatchet and buried it in a tree. He was like a caged animal, trapped and ready to lash out.

Tamoset was glad none of the other braves could see this. They knew nothing of Canonchet's death. All they had heard was that the warriors had a string of victories, ending with the burning of Providence. Now they were celebrating. They need to dance, thought Tamoset. They need to feel good.

Philip was pacing. He exclaimed angrily one last time, then looked up at the evening sky. The western horizon was streaked with red, reminding him of the bloody work that still lay ahead. The April night was balmy, the first real hint of warmth in five months.

Philip was calmer now. He asked, "How could he let himself get caught? Why was he with so few braves?"

Tamoset only shook his head. There was really no more he could say. Canonchet was the chief of the largest group of warriors, and he did what he did for his own reasons. There was nothing anyone could do to change what had happened.

Tamoset unconciously rubbed his shoulder. He had a festering wound there that would not heal, having been hit accidentally by one of his own braves when the smoke of a burning building had obscured friend and foe. Fortunately, the arrow was almost spent when it hit.

Philip noticed, softened, and said, "Tend to your wound. We have much to do in the days ahead."

"The wound is nothing," said Tamoset. Then he hesitated and said, "Philip, wait until morning to tell the others. Let them have their celebration. They fought well, and seven more English towns are in ashes."

Philip nodded and walked toward his wigwam.

Tamoset was relieved to see him go, but a great loneliness settled upon him. He had just arrived back at the camp, and had nowhere to go, no one to talk to. His family was gone, and most of his friends were either on the warpath or dead. Philip was his closest friend, and now he was becoming unapproachable as the war dragged on.

We need to strike Boston, thought Tamoset. We need the big victory to make the tribes who have stayed out of the conflict join our side.

He wandered over to the celebration, and watched from a distance. A huge fire roared and around it braves pantomimed their battle actions. All chanted to the battle spirit, a welcoming call, a call of companionship. The rhythm of the drum went faster and faster. Men raised their tomahawks toward the east, toward Plymouth and Boston.

One Narragansett man outperformed all the others. He leaped high into the air, then swooped low and pounded the earth. Sweat glistened from his arms, and his hair flew wildly behind him. Around his neck was a necklace of cougar claws that the other braves eyed with envy. His body and face were streaked erratically with yellow and red war paint, giving him a fierce glow. Suddenly he stopped his dance, raised both arms to the sky, and let out a bloodcurdling scream.

Tamoset allowed himself a bitter smile. He knew the rage the brave felt, and he was glad to see it expressed so perfectly. If only the others can keep that hatred at a fever pitch, we will win this war, he thought. We are close now. The whites have fled to their bigger towns, leaving the countryside to us. They are weakening and show little enthusiasm for taking to the trail.

While Tamoset stood in the shadows, he heard a baby cry from a wigwam nearby. The sound woke him from his ruminations, and he decided he needed someone to talk to. Ochala was the only person he trusted. The old man had always been there to listen. It no longer mattered that Ochala and he were from different tribes; both tended to look at things analytically, and both were lonely deep down. They understood one another even though they often disagreed.

Tamoset walked toward Ochala and Quinna's wigwam. He had not seen either of them since before the journey to Canonchet. On his way, he passed the wigwam where the baby had cried.

After Tamoset had passed by, the baby inside the wigwam cried and fussed again. He was not getting enough breast milk from the woman who had been caring for him. But he was a strong child, tenacious and stubborn, just like his father, who had just passed outside but had no idea he was alive.

Chapter 28

Quinna greeted Tamoset at the wigwam opening and invited him in. He noticed she looked tired, the normal spark in her black eyes was not there. But she was still beautiful and still exuded a cat-like grace. Tamoset seated himself across from her on the other side of the small fire.

"It is good to see you," said Tamoset. He rubbed the top of his head, fingers going through the bristle where he had not found the time to shave around his scalplock. He knew he looked awful.

"I am glad you made it back safe. I hear the warriors dancing and singing outside. Another victory?"

"Providence is burned; so are many other towns."

Quinna nodded and poked at the fire. Tamoset wondered where Ochala could be, because the old man was not the type to join in celebrations.

"Where is your father?"

"He's gone on. He died two weeks ago."

Tamoset's eyes narrowed, pulling his head back as if being hit.

Quinna continued, voice wavering. "He told me to say goodbye to you. He said he would talk to you again on the other side."

Tamoset was shocked. He knew the old man had been sick, but had no idea how serious. His first thought was selfish—now I have no one, now I am truly alone. He looked directly at her, saw the anguish in her eyes, then looked away quickly. Silence. He stared into the yellow flames.

"How did he die?"

"From cold, hunger, too much moving from camp to camp."

Tamoset nodded; it really should not have surprised him. Many of the old and very young had died, the indirect casualties of the war. He thought of Ochala the first day they met and remembered how his thin, wiry arms hacked at the pine log, shaping it into a canoe. He saw his white hair swaying to and fro with each chop, his wrinkled old face concentrating on the task. He remembered how he gave him orders: "Steady the canoe. Drop chips on the coals," and so on. Tamoset first thought he was cold and crusty; only later did he warm to Ochala's direct manner.

He had not noticed that Quinna had stood and poured water from a clay pot. Now she handed him a cup. Her eyes were moist, but her voice was back in control, saying, "Ochala liked you. He said you had much wisdom for such a young man."

Tamoset smiled bitterly, shaking his head. He didn't feel young and certainly not wise. Silence again, longer this time, awkward. He rose to his feet, turned to go, saying, "He will not be forgotten."

Quinna remained seated, but abruptly said, "Stay for a moment, tell me of the battles."

Tamoset hesitated, then sat again. He was glad for the chance to talk, even if about the war.

He told her first about Medfield, how they hid in the farmer's barn but somehow they were spotted. He told her the farmer might have been the same one who shot him in the face months earlier, giving him the scar. He detailed how he chased him into the garrison, laying siege to the building but was never successful in burning it.

It was there that he came to realize that attacking well-fortified garrisons was wasting too many braves. He explained how he told Philip this, but that his friend would not listen, such was his contempt for the whites.

She watched him talk, listening, happy just to hear another voice. Since Ochala had died she stayed mostly in her wigwam. Occasionally Mary Rowlandson would come by, bringing firewood. She would give the English woman chestnuts or a bit of turnip, and Rowlandson would sit by her fire warming herself. But they did not talk, could not even if they wanted to because the language was so different and the customs so strange.

Now she soaked up his words, encouraging him by nodding or asking a question here and there. For the first time she realized what a brave man he was. He had fought in many battles, never resting in between for more than a day or two.

She looked at him closely. The scar made him appear ugly at first glance. His face was stoic, never giving a hint at his emotion. But up close, one only had to look at his eyes. They were sad eyes, deep eyes, eyes that mirrored what was in his soul. She had seen them with a crazed look the time he returned with the other warriors, running into camp triumphantly after the Medfield raid. But she had also seen them at a happier time, before the pain of loosing his family.

She remembered the time at the Connecticut River camp when he had chipped the stone and given it to the little girl. And then she recalled how she saw the eyes look so confused the first time they met, the time she was swimming when she accused him of spying on her.

He is special, she thought, not like the others; he treats me with respect and kindness, the same as he did my father. And he is a warrior, never boasting, never caring about his own safety. She looked at his lips, wondered what it would be like to kiss him, looked at his hands and wished they would hold her and comfort her in the lonliness she felt to her core.

Tamoset let the words tumble out. He described how they set each building in Providence ablaze, but that when they got to Roger William's house, Canonchet said to leave it. He told her how much he wanted to burn that house, how he almost did in spite of Canonchet.

Canonchet's name caused him to shake his head, telling her how important he was. He was to have been the southern leader, Muttawmp to the west, and Philip would have stayed north attacking the towns north and west of Boston. Then Tamoset surprised himself by confiding in her about Philip's outburst when he told him of Canonchet's death.

"Why do you stay with him?" asked Quinna. "Why not fight with Muttawmp along the Great River to the west?"

It was difficult to answer. His own wife had asked him the same question many times. Why do I follow him? He thought of Philip, thought of his temper; he even blamed me for

Canonchet's death. Philip. It was impossible to think of him without the picture of the ambush at Deerfield coming to mind—fearlessly flying through the air at the soldiers, killing many with his bare hands.

He knew Philip had his own demons, knew that deep down he must have had his own doubts, but above all knew he was a man of honor. Philip was not a perfect man, but a man of vision, a natural leader. Not to lead his people at a time like this would be the easy way out. But how could he explain the man to Quinna? He tried.

"Philip is my friend—he has been like an older brother to me. As children we played together, Philip always daring me to do more, always free with his knowledge, showing me a better way. He is a great man, yes, but he has another side. You have never seen him play with his young son. He would throw the boy far into the air, so far a normal boy would cry, but not his son. His father always caught him and told him someday he would fly like the hawk. How the boy's eyes sparkled, believing that any day he would sprout wings! Yes, Philip made him feel important, just as he makes all of us feel that way. Remember how he took the time to talk to the woman captive, telling her he would pay her for her labor? He respected her courage; it made no difference that she was white. He is different than the rest of us."

He had not intended to say so much, embarrassed that he had. The wigwam was warm, and he took off his cape.

Quinna saw a patch of dried blood on his shoulder and the unhealed wound beneath.

"I'll get something for that," she said, standing. She went to a basket in the back of the wigwam and fished through it, selecting the proper medicinal herbs. Then she returned and sat beside him.

His pulse quickened. He could smell her sweetness, marveling at the sheen in her hair. As she cleaned the wound he looked at her fingers. They were so long and graceful, yet strong and sure. When she looked up at him and asked how he got the wound, he saw the sadness in her eyes.

He felt weak having her so close. She was more beautiful than he had thought. He struggled to find his voice.

"Happened at Providence," he said huskily.

She nodded and continued working, now applying the herbs to the wound.

Just being this near her was arousing him. He wanted to escape, felt trapped, knew he would have to leave as soon as she was finished. He remembered all too well what happened the night he kissed her.

The silence was deafening. He forced himself to talk.

"Ochala was one of the few people I could talk to. When I met him I first thought him rude. He spoke directly, saying we could not win the war. I was mad at first, but later learned that was his manner. I remember how surprised I was when he smiled the day I gave him that bear meat. After that I looked forward to seeing him."

He said all this staring into the fire, not noticing that Quinna was done with his shoulder. He turned and looked at her. Tears were streaming down her face.

His hand went out, as if controlled by someone else, and touched her cheek, lightly brushing a tear.

She did not withdraw, but looked into his eyes and saw his concern. She saw something more, saw the tribe, not just her tribe but all the people. She could see the inner strength, but could also see the flames. The haunting sight made her shudder. She felt a power in the room.

She ran her hand along the scar of his face. Suddenly, as if a wall of water washed over her, she felt a love for this man. Why and where it came from she did not know, did not care. She only wanted to protect him. Through the tears she smiled, thinking to herself; this is what I've been waiting for, this is the man.

She took her hand from his face and stood up. The flames of the fire had died down to a flicker, casting a dim yellow light on her. First she pulled one side of her doeskin dress off one shoulder then the other. The dress slowly dropped to her waist.

Tamoset's eyes widened, staring up at her, breathing heavily. The day at the river came rushing back to him, the day he saw her naked from a distance. He was stunned then, and he was stunned now, only this time she was three feet away.

She pulled her dress down the rest of the way and stood before him. Her arms came out, and she extended her hands toward him.

When he took her hands a charge went through his body. It was the first touch of warmth he had since Napatoo. His eyes grew moist. He sat as if in a trance, still staring but not moving.

She gently tugged at his hand, pulling him up from his sitting position. Now they were standing face to face, close enough to feel the breath of the other. She lightly ran her fingers down his chest and felt him tremble. Then she lay her hands flat against his chest feeling his strength.

It still seemed like a dream to him, but now there was a roaring in his ears. He responded by cupping her breasts, amazed at the softness of her skin. She was so smooth, as smooth as polished wampum, and he rubbed her, stroked her like a sacred stone.

She pulled him forward, wrapping her arms around him, feeling his hardness and the heat of his body. She held him tighter, heard him exhale slowly and deeply. She felt his lips on her neck, his hands slowly running down her back. There was a flutter in her belly, and her knees grew weak.

Neither could stand the excitement anymore, and together they lay on the furs, becoming one, holding as tightly as they could, rocking in spasms of pure joy.

Chapter 29

He came back at last from that faraway place, one arm still holding her slim waist. His muscles slowly uncoiled, and a deep languor settled on him. But he did not want sleep to come, did not want to drift off from her, not yet.

Tamoset watched her laying there, eyes closed, black hair spread out on the beaver skins. She was on her side, one of her arms draped over his chest like a cougar on its prey. Yes, he thought, she is a strong cat. He breathed deeply of her scent. A thin braid of hair was on one side of her head, and he studied it closely, wanting to remember every detail.

With his free arm he was able to reach the little pile of sticks and feed the glowing coals. In a matter of seconds tiny flames were licking at the new wood, and he enjoyed watching the progress of the fire. It seemed that in spite of the thousands of wigwam fires he had started, this, he thought, was the first he had ever really seen. Fire, you too are my friend, he said to himself.

Intuitively he knew the cloud of darkness had lifted. He would still fight, still try to drive the invaders out, but no longer would he make suicidal charges. He had something to live for, someone living to fight for in addition to those that were gone.

He thought of Napatoo and Chusett and the happy days on Montaup. He could see her feeding Chusett with the glow of contentment on her face.

Tears flowed uncontrollably; now he could finally mourn their deaths freely. And as he silently wept, he could feel the misery of his winter anguish slowly dissolve. He knew his family was in a better place, knew he would see them again on the other side.

He felt Quinna stir, saw her open her eyes with a look of concern on her face.

"Why the tears?" she whispered.

"Tears of joy," he lied.

"I feel it too. For the first time I feel whole." She rolled to her stomach, propped her head on her elbows and looked into the fire with him. "To think that love still exists amongst so much suffering," she mused.

He nodded.

They watched the flames silently together; then Tamoset said, "It is late, you should sleep now."

She shook her head no, her hand finding his. Later they made love again, this time slowly, gently, with whispers.

* * * *

A whiff of food coming through the wigwam's opening awakened Tamoset in the morning. He rolled over to put his arm around Quinna, but she was gone. He sat up quickly, wondering what this meant. Did she regret the night, did she want to be alone?

He put on his breach clout and leggings and then stepped outside. Quinna was there sitting with Mary Rowlandson, and both women were shelling nuts. Quinna looked up at him smiling, and Tamoset felt a joy well up inside; it would be all right; the words spoken in passion were true.

The day was warmer than the one before, and the whole camp was out and about. For the first time Tamoset realized just how big this camp was. He feared the whites might learn of it, and he decided to tell Philip to post more lookouts farther out.

Rowlandson kept her eyes on her work, but she could tell Tamoset was staring at her. She feared him more than the others; maybe it was the scar, maybe the smouldering in his eyes, but the last time she saw him she could feel the hatred exuding from him.

And now this man had shared the wigwam with Quinna, the one woman who had showed her kindness, perhaps saving her from starvation. She said a silent prayer, "Lord be my strength, do not let them send me back to my mistress. I cannot cross the wilderness again."

Tamoset sat down next to Quinna, still staring at Rowlandson, amazed at the paleness of her skin and the sky-colored eyes.

"What is her name?" he asked Quinna.

"She says it is *Mar-ri*. She was taken from the town they call Lancaster some time ago. Her baby recently died, and her other children are captives, taken to the west."

Tamoset considered this for a moment, his feelings softening a bit. He had much to ask her, but could not say the strange, harsh sounds the English made, and neither could Quinna. If he could, he would ask why her people steal native land, why they massacred women and children at the Great

Swamp camp when the Narragansetts had not taken to the warpath. But mostly he wanted to know why these strangers who landed on his shore had forgotten the kindness of Massasoit and his father.

"She has courage," said Quinna. "She complains little and does what she can to help. She reads her book of magic, the book of her god. Ochala told me that the whites think that their god is the only god, and ours are not real. At first I was going to throw her book into the fire, but I saw how it comforted her. She does not seem evil."

Tamoset shrugged. "I do not know." He cast another glance at Rowlandson, sizing her up. Then in a low voice, he continued, "Perhaps she is not as evil as the rest, but maybe her husband was the one who killed my wife and son. Who can say? You know the whites have been plotting for years to be rid of us. They had most of the Wampanoag land, but still they wanted it all. I have never seen such greed in any of the tribes. My father told me that even when we fought the Narragansetts many seasons ago, the Narragansetts did not take our land, even though they were stronger."

Rowlandson was growing more nervous by the minute. She could not understand the exchange between the two, but it was clear they were talking about her. Lord, do not let him raise the hatchet, not now, I have suffered so.

She focused on shelling the nuts but her heart was racing, causing her to be light-headed. To calm herself she thought of her favorite passage from the Scripture, repeating over and over: "Cast thy burden upon thy Lord and he shall sustain thee."

Quinna put her hand on Tamoset's knee, "I understand what you say. Still this woman is just one person. When you were attacking Providence, I was with the white woman when she gave Philip the cap she had made for his son. Philip took her hand and spoke to her. He then turned to me, saying, 'I told her that in just a few moons she will be her own mistress again.' He said he was sending word to the whites that they could buy her freedom."

Tamoset was confused. Philip directs the attacks, does not seem concerned over the braves we lose when attacking garrisons because he wants every single white dead. And yet here is this woman that he will let go free for a few shillings. His thoughts were interrupted by Quinna's hailing of a passing friend.

"Come here, Squannock, let us see how the little boy fares."

The woman approached, cradling the baby in a soft blanket of doeskin. Quinna stood to look at the child. Tamoset hesitated, then did the same.

Squannock pulled the doeskin back, and the boy squirmed to get free, turning his face toward Tamoset and Quinna.

Tamoset gasped. He stepped back and tried to talk, but only a grunt came out.

"What is it?" cried Quinna, grabbing his arm.

The color had drained from his face. On wobbly knees he stepped forward, staring at the boy. Leaning down, his face just inches from the boy's, he whispered something. Quinna put her head next to his, straining to hear.

Tamoset whispered again to the baby, "It's you." He turned to Quinna, eyes misted over, "It is my son."

Chapter 30

"All right men, it's finally time, time to give them red devils a surprise."

Captain Turner stopped for a moment, hacking and coughing uncontrollably. His face was yellowish, and his clothes hung loosely on a bony frame.

Homer watched the Captain closely, but still knew this was the man to lead them. In spite of Turner's obvious illness, his voice had an authoritative quality to it, one that could give men confidence if the going got rough.

Alongside Homer stood almost 150 men, each waiting silently for Turner to continue. They were gathered inside the palisade walls of the garrison at Hadley, the colony's westernmost outpost.

Turner looked like he might collapse, and Homer was about to step forward to assist him when he steadied, and the coughing subsided.

"Men, I've been as tired of this damn guard duty as you have. But now Boston has agreed to let me carry out my plan. Not only that, but now I know exactly where the red devils have their village. The freed captive boy who entered the garrison last night gave us much information. The heathens have a huge camp, just twenty miles up the river by the great falls. He says there are hundreds of Injuns there, and a great stock of provisions and ..." He started hacking again, back bent and head bowed low.

When the coughing subsided and he lifted his head, Homer could see the sweat dripping from his forehead. He must have a terrible fever, thought Homer.

Indeed, Turner had been sick for months. Now it was mid-May and the trees were leafing out, yet he felt like it was August, the fever burned in him so badly. But the news from the boy captive gave him the strength to leave his sickbed. The boy had said the natives posted no guards; such was their contempt for the whites.

Turner found his voice again, "Make no mistake about it, this will be extremely dangerous for us. Step out now if you have no guts for this."

Homer looked up and down the line of men, then to the other rows behind. Not a soldier or farmer moved. Turner stood nodding, a grim smile on his white lips.

"Sir, we're with you," a local farmer spoke up from the rear, "I reckon if we are going to get our fields planted this spring we best get on with it."

Turner gave a weak smile, and the men murmured their approval.

"We march at dusk. Captain Holyoke will assist me, and John Homer and George Oliver will act as scouts with the Praying Indians."

Homer was not surprised; he had spoken with Turner many times, sharing his experiences at the Great Swamp and the Medfield attack. Through all of April, Homer had pleaded with

Turner to take the offensive, but Turner had said he must wait for Boston to approve his plan.

It was a frustrating period for Homer, cooped up in the garrison knowing the natives were prowling the countryside. In the east they had recently attacked Worcester, Sudbury, Groton and Marlborough. Here in the west they continued to lie in ambush for farmers foolish enough to risk returning to their fields. And just one week ago a large band of warriors hit the Hadley garrison at dawn, killing three soldiers and taking over seventy head of cattle.

The garrison was terribly isolated, with only an occasional patrol arriving from Springfield. Food was low, and Homer was sick of the thin soup and moldy bread. And as each day passed, he grew more worried about his family, wondering what was happening back in Medfield. He grew so cross he even went to Turner and asked to be dismissed so he could head home and fight there. But Turner said no, telling him to hang on, that there would soon be plenty enough action right here.

Now Turner dismissed the men, telling them to bring only their muskets and to be ready to march at sundown.

Homer was elated; finally, we are taking to the field, he thought, doing what Ben Church had been advocating for months.

Oliver walked back to the barracks alongside Homer.

"John, I sure wish I had a spot of ale to partake with you. Never know if we're going to make it out of this one."

" 'Twill be a mean scrap for sure, but I've got faith in Turner, Holyoke too for that matter. They are not afraid, and once they commit they move fast."

"Now that's the spirit. Never know, maybe I'll see old King Philip himself at the end of my musket and be the richest man in the colonies."

Homer didn't laugh; he scratched the stubble on his chin and thought of Philip. "What I would give," said Homer, "to just have him within range. Kill him, and all the Indians would break up into so many pieces."

* * * *

Holyoke and Turner were on horseback, but the rest of the men followed behind on foot, moving swiftly, silently, not a word exchanged for over fifteen miles. The only provisions each carried was a handful of cornmeal in his pockets, which each hoped to mix with a bit of water on the return march.

Homer, Oliver and the two Praying Indians, Masquam and One-eyed Sam, scouted the trail ahead. Homer had one of the men in the rear carry his musket, preferring to hold an Indian tomahawk on this night-time mission. He figured it was so dark, the musket would do no good, while the tomahawk was the perfect weapon for hand-to-hand fighting.

Masquam raised his hand for the others to stop. He leaned toward Homer.

"Tell Captain we close, be there before morning sun. Tell men not make sound, could lose scalp. Go quick."

Homer hated taking orders from an Indian, but he went back down the trail alone to tell Turner they would be at the village soon. He wondered what Masquam would do once the fighting started. Maybe he will melt into the woods, keeping himself from harm. Perhaps, he thought with a stab of fear, perhaps all along he has just pretended to help us, gaining our trust only to deliver us into a waiting swarm of warriors.

A chill ran down his spine, thinking what would happen if he were taken alive. As much as he wanted to take this bold action, he had a nagging apprehension. If the captive boy was incorrect in his assessment that the camp was unguarded, we're as good as dead, he worried.

He whistled softly when he could hear the men and the horses, he didn't want them to mistake him for a hostile Indian and shoot. Turner came up on his horse, Holyoke by his side.

"What is it, John?"

"Sir, the Indian scout says we are almost there. He wants you to tell the men not to make a sound."

"Good, the sun will be up in a few minutes; we must be in place before the savages are up. When you see the village, just wait on the trail; I'll have the men fan out and form a semicircle around the camp. No one fires till I give the order. But remember, even if they have guards posted, we're going in. We didn't come this far to turn tail."

"Yes sir, and God be with you, sir."

Homer jogged back up the trail and joined Oliver and the scouts.

Oliver cupped a hand around his mouth and whispered in Homer's ear, "Stay by me John, we can watch each other's back."

They walked slowly now, ears straining for any unusual sound. Once an owl hooted, but the two Christian Indians didn't even stop, obviously convinced that it was the real thing. The outlines of the trees seemed to stand out a bit more, and

Homer knew that the night's blackness was fading and being replaced by the charcoal grey of false dawn.

Fifteen more minutes of walking and Masquam slowed to a crawl, lifted his arm and pointed straight ahead. Homer could see nothing up the path, nor hear anything, and he wondered if the man was mistaken.

They moved ahead silently, and Homer was surprised to hear a distant wind. How could that be; there wasn't even the slightest breeze? Then he realized it was not the wind, but the muffled sound of falling water, the great falls at the Connecticut River.

Fifty more feet and he thought he caught a whiff of wood smoke, and seconds later he smelled something different in the dank air. There were butterflies in his stomach, and unconsciously he gripped the tomahawk with all his might. Now he recognized the smell; it was fish, salmon he thought.

Masquam motioned for the men to stop. He pointed at Homer, then at the ground. This meant that Homer should stay there and wait for Holyoke; the perimeter of the village must be just a few feet ahead.

Homer watched as Oliver slipped to the left, One-eyed Sam to the right, and Masquam glided straight ahead, disappearing into the shadowy haze. Homer's heart was pounding; any minute he expected to hear a war whoop or the crack of a musket.

He stood silently, his mind racing over every detail. How could he fight with Oliver if he didn't even know where he was? God, what if Turner was still on his horse, what if the animal snorted and gave away their position? I better go back a little, better intercept Turner before they get any closer.

Homer breathed a sigh of relief when he saw Turner on foot, the men stretched behind him in single file. After giving the whistle, Homer showed himself and went to Turner's side.

"Captain," he whispered in a low voice, "the village is just beyond these trees."

"Good, the Injuns are just where the boy said, right above the falls. Captain Holyoke, get the men in position. Make sure they understand that every other man shoots on the first order. The rest wait and fire at escaping Indians; then we charge."

Holyoke passed Homer a musket, and then sent word back among the troops to load weapons, spread out, take positions at the edge of the clearing, and wait for Turner's command.

Homer stayed with Turner as they made their way to the edge of the trees. In dawn's grey light they could see hundreds of wigwams, stretched out like the domes of muskrat lodges on a marsh, covering the western bank of the river. A steep rock cliff rose from the far end of the village, providing a windbreak for the camp.

Minutes passed. Homer knew that Turner was waiting for just a bit more light to expose the targets better. Now, he could see the outline of prone bodies of those who preferred to sleep in the open. Along the river, canoes were beached. Above the charcoal remains of fires were wooden racks used to smoke fish. With each passing second more details of the camp came into focus, and Homer was amazed at its size; there must be 500 people here, he thought.

He looked at Turner, but the captain was staring ahead, as if stunned by the size of the village. Seconds crawled by. Now, Homer thought, we should attack now, don't wait any longer. His hands were clammy on the musket, and he took his finger off the trigger, not trusting himself during this agonizing wait.

Homer's eyes widened. A woman was already up feeding a fire, and a dog trotted at her side. What is he waiting for? We are doomed if we lose the advantage of surprise. Homer reached out and touched Turner on the sleeve.

Turner's sunken eyes stared back at Homer, a vacant, hollow look to them. Oh God, thought Homer in a panic, he's gone mad, his illness is clouding his judgment, he can't—

"Fire!" screamed Turner, splitting the air until the muskets roared in response.

A cloud of musket smoke blocked Homer's vision. He could hear cries and screams from ahead. He thought he heard shouts of, "Mohawks! Mohawks!" mixed with the terrified shrieks. Then the smoke drifted off, and he could see natives fleeing from their wigwams, running every which way, not knowing where the enemy was.

"Fire again!" Turner bellowed, voice cracking.

This time Homer saw scores drop.

The English were on their feet charging into the camp. Some chased natives toward the river, and others went to the wigwams pointing muskets directly inside before discharging.

Homer reloaded and ran to the riverbank. Already there were many natives swimming madly in the water; others were diving into the canoes and paddling furiously to get to the other side. The English lined the banks and fired time and time again. Canoes overturned, spilling all into the swift current. Within seconds they were swept over the falls like so much flotsam. Some tried to swim under water, but musket balls were waiting when they surfaced.

The camp proved to be a trap of death. Those that ran north and west had to scale the steep rock embankment, and many were shot as they climbed, while the roaring river hemmed them in on the east. There was no escape; the river, the wall of rock and the English had them trapped. The carnage was over in a matter of minutes. Only a few were taken alive as prisoners.

Turner stood at the center of camp. "Men, fire the wigwams, throw any supplies you find into the river. Be quick about it."

Homer took a burning stick from a campfire and put it to the nearest wigwam. A massive cloud of smoke rose, and he thought to himself, this is the Great Swamp all over again.

Except for the crackle of wigwams burning, there was an eerie silence where just minutes before the musket fire had been deafening. He noticed some of the men were sitting down, gorging themselves on food found in some of the wigwams. They ate among the dead bodies, not caring that their feet rested in blood.

"Look! Across the river!" shouted Homer, pointing. Warriors could be seen along the opposite shore.

Turner looked and, although separated by the river, felt threatened. The attack had been a total success, but he knew his small army was still twenty miles from the nearest garrison.

"All right, we're moving out!" he barked.

One of the captured Indians sneered and spoke in halting English, "Philip and a thousand warriors come."

Those close enough to hear this moved out quickly, but others were slow to get in line, trying to carry baskets of corn.

"Leave the corn, damn you! Get in line!" screamed Turner. "Oliver! Homer! To the front with the Christian Indians!"

Homer and Oliver ran to One-eyed Sam and Masquam.

Masquam had a worried look on his face as he gazed across the river, then scanned the top of the cliff.

"Me no like this. Make mistake when burn wigwams, smoke send signal to nearby warriors of trouble."

Now it was Homer's turn to worry; this was the most he had ever heard Masquam say, and all of it was bad. They began the march, moving as quickly as their exhausted legs would carry them. None of the men had slept, most had not eaten, and all had been on their feet for over twelve hours.

Shafts of sunlight filtered through the giant pines, and ferns grew along the woodland trail. The morning was warming up, and Homer was thirsty, but he didn't dare veer from the path. They walked quickly, following the same trail that had carried them north during the night; only this time they could see where they were going.

They passed the charred remains of a settler's cabin, the skeletal remains of the family probably somewhere under the ashes. After a half-hour Homer began to relax, knowing that with every step they were getting closer to Hadley. He shifted his gaze from the trail ahead to the side, searching for signs of an ambush.

Then all hell broke loose. Blood-chilling war whoops came from the rear, and the soldiers stampeded ahead as arrows fell among them. Homer tried to stop them, fearful they would run right into a bigger ambush, but the men flew by in total disarray. They had seen braves charging up the trail like an angry swarm of bees, everyone fearful that it was Philip and a thousand warriors the prisoner had warned of.

Captain Holyoke rode up, trying to stop the retreat, but the men ignored him, charging past like horses fleeing a fire.

"Stop damn you!" he screamed, waving his sword. "Form a line!"

But the men kept running.

Homer ran to Holyoke. "Where's Captain Turner?" he shouted.

"Dead! I need your help, John! Grab some of these men, we've got to stay together!"

Together, Homer, Holyoke and Oliver slowed a few men down and formed them into a line. No sooner had they done so than the braves came pouring down the path. The soldiers discharged their muskets, instantly killing the first six, while the others broke from the trail for the protection of the trees.

"Fall back!" cried Holyoke, "We have a chance to catch the others and form another line further down the trail."

With Holyoke in the lead on his horse, they followed him, dashing ahead, hoping to overtake more soldiers before the braves regrouped. Some of the men who had panicked before had now come to their senses and were waiting. Holyoke kept them moving, hoping they would arrive at another clearing that would be easier to defend.

Minutes went by, and not another brave was seen. Holyoke kept the men moving, wondering where the natives would attack from next.

Just as the soldiers began to cross a small river, the braves sprang from the woods and charged, seeming to come from all directions. Holyoke's horse was hit with an arrow and both horse and rider crashed to the ground. A brave charged forward, tomahawk raised, to finish Holyoke off.

In the slow motion that men often witness in battle, Homer saw his friend in trouble and screamed, "Behind you!"

Holyoke sprang to his feet, drew his sword and lashed out at the warrior, beheading him instantly.

In the confusion, some soldiers ran blindly up the path, right into waiting warriors, while others tried to follow the riverbank away from the center of the fighting. The English had lost all order; now it was every man for himself.

Homer was behind a fallen log with Masquam firing at the braves across the river. The air was heavy with musket smoke, and he lost sight of Holyoke. Just a few feet away he saw Oliver crumple to the ground with an arrow in his gut. Homer said a silent prayer and prepared to die.

"Only one way to save ourselves," said Masquam.

"How?" asked Homer, ramming another lead ball into his musket. "We haven't long before they are on us."

"We trick them. I will strip out of this English shirt. Maybe in the smoke they will think I am one of them. Then I chase you into the woods as if to kill you. Then we both run away."

It took Homer just a second to see the wisdom of this plan, a plan that just might save his life. There was no other option.

"Yes, it might work. Let's slide down to the end of the log, then we go."

Masqaum took off the shirt and picked up his tomahawk. When they reached the end of the log, Homer took a deep breath and then he started running with Masquam right behind him, tomahawk raised.

The natives on the other side watched without firing, wondering who this warrior was. Then one of them screamed, "It's a traitor, white-man brave, white-man brave!"

All at once the warriors let fly their arrows, three of them hitting Masquam in the back just as he reached the thicker trees away from the riverbank.

Homer skidded to a stop and looked back at Musquam who waved him on. There was no choice; if he stopped to help they would both be killed. He ran on. Behind him he could hear the warriors charging across the river, screaming at the top of their lungs, coming for him like wolves running down a deer.

He crashed through branches, running wildly, expecting an arrow in his back at any minute. He could see a clearing through the foliage and he ran toward it. His lungs screamed with pain, and knew he could not keep up the sprint for much longer. At the clearing he decided; instead of running across it, he turned to his left, ran a few feet, then dove into thick brush.

He could hear the braves coming on his trail. They stopped suddenly. They glanced at the ground but their was no time to study for footprints; if they were going to catch this soldier and still get the others, they must act quickly. Two warriors went directly across the tiny clearing, the logical route Homer would have followed, but the third walked around the edge of the clearing peering into the woods.

Homer debated weather to spring up and flee again, but decided against it. A soft rattling noise came from nearby, inches from his head. Slowly he turned and saw the snake, a rattler, curled beneath a granite boulder. Every instinct in Homer's being told him to flee, but he knew the brave was near; one sudden move and the warrior might hear him.

With his head flat on the ground, he could look right into the snake's eyes, see its tongue flashing. He didn't move a muscle. Then he heard talking in the clearing; the two who had run through the field had returned, and now all three were talking. He had no idea what they were saying, but knew his life depended on the outcome of their decision. If they come toward me, he thought, I will throw myself on the snake—better to die of snake poison than to be taken alive.

Seconds went by. His heart was beating so loud he was afraid they might hear it. Then the warriors started running, but not toward him; they were going back to the river, going to kill other white soldiers.

Homer did not move. He lay there for hours, muscles cramped, occasionally glancing at the snake. His mouth felt like cotton had been stuffed in it. In mid-afternoon the snake slithered off, but Homer stayed where he was. It wasn't until darkness had fallen that he stood and took his first steps south.

Chapter 31

"Will you tell me what happened now?" Quinna asked softly, not wishing to anger Tamoset on his return from the warpath. They were sitting by a waterfall, a full two miles from camp, a secret place Quinna had found while searching for food. Chusett was with them, his face smeared with red juice from the strawberries he was gobbling down.

Tamoset nodded but said nothing. He was watching the water, thinking how beautiful this spot was, how soothing the sound of splashing water. If I stay here long enough, maybe I can forget the war.

"We were successful, the braves fought hard. Many farms were burned in the town they call Sudbury. When the English soldiers came for us we were waiting. After all this time they still look straight ahead, never to the side, never thinking ambush. They were all soldiers, no native cowards who pray to the white man's God. We killed many."

"Then why are you unhappy?"

"I'm not unhappy."

"Yes, something is wrong."

"Nothing is wrong; I just have a bad feeling about things."

"Tamoset, you can tell me. Is not our love so great that we can talk straight?"

"Yes, we can always talk; you understand things others do not."

He stroked Chusett's head, and the baby smiled. The fact that the baby was alive was almost beyond Tamoset's comprehension. Did the Great Spirit intervene? How could this child be alive when all the others were killed?

He had spent many nights lying awake wondering what had happened that allowed his son to be the only living thing found inside the Great Swamp Camp. The Narragansett woman who cared for the baby all winter said only that a boy brought the baby to her. But she did not know how it came about that the baby was alive, only that there must be something special about one who lives where others die. The woman thought the Great Spirit had singled out the boy.

Quinna brought Tamoset out of his ruminations by asking again, "If you destroyed the English town, why the bad feelings?"

Tamoset swatted a mosquito away, thinking how to answer.

"It is difficult to explain. Yes, we won a great victory, but still I did not return victorious. We should have done much more. We should have struck again, closer to Boston. There are many towns that have not been touched. I told the braves we must go on, but most said no. Most said they needed to rest, needed to catch fish on their upstream journey. The braves are tired, hungry, but that is no excuse. They grow soft. Some even talk of peace."

"The women are the same. All they talk about is returning to the fields to plant. Many curse Philip behind his back."

"That is what I mean; there are bad signs."

"But there have been bad signs before. Remember at the Great River Camp how a few braves slipped out before the snow winds came?"

Tamoset nodded tiredly. The mention of the camp by the Great River made him think of Ponotuck. A chill went down his spine as he recalled how Philip confronted his sleeping friend the morning he was killed. Did Ponotuck trade talk to the English for the shiny metal? He would never know for sure.

Quinna continued, "You still think we will destroy the English, don't you? Even Ochala thought so at the end."

"Sometimes the signs are good; sometimes they disturb me. We kill so many English, we burn so many towns, yet there are always more."

"Maybe they keep coming across the Great Water in their big-canoes-with-cloth. It seems as if the wind pushes them here. Why our country?" Quinna asked rhetorically.

Tamoset stared at the falls—they come like the river water, always more. Nothing can stop the river, can we stop the whites?

They were silent for a time, each thinking their own thoughts. Some were best left unsaid. Chusett had fallen asleep. The forest was still except for the occasional call of a bluejay or cardinal.

Tamoset ate from the basket of strawberries enjoying their sweetness, but he needed something more filling; there was always a hunger in his belly.

Quinna broke the silence, asking the question she had been thinking about for some time, "What will happen to us? Will we ever be able to stop the fighting?"

Tamoset shrugged. He did not know what the future would bring. He knew the whites would never be driven into the ocean; the best he hoped for now was to hurt them badly enough so they might leave the land in the west to the natives.

"Try not to think of tomorrow."

Quinna studied his face, "You are tired, Tamoset, you push yourself too hard. You cannot go on every raid. Let some of the others go. Some have stayed at the camp for many moons without taking to the warpath, yet you never rest here."

"The men you speak of are weak, no, they are cowards, they let others go in their place. I do not want them with me. When they do go on raids they are of little good. They stay to the rear as the battle increases, shooting arrows that wobble by the time they reach the whites. They are afraid of the death call, afraid of the white's God."

"Tamoset," said Quinna sharply, "You may not care if you die, but I do."

He looked at her, saw her mouth set firm. He touched her face and shook his head. "I do care. I do not want to die, not now, not since we became one. But I am not afraid to be killed. I cannot control that—when it's time, the Creator will call."

Quinna knew that this was true, knew that this was the core of the man; he was not afraid and never had been. She put her arms around him and held tightly.

"I understand, but still you have been wounded twice, need some rest. Even a wounded bird knows to lie still, even a wounded bird lets time pass."

"I do what I must."

"Still, think twice before you go on the next raid; even Philip does not go on every one. Think of your son, he needs you now."

Her words had a haunting ring of what Napatoo had spoken before the trouble started. What she says makes sense, thought Tamoset. I do need to rest, I can tell my strength is fading. But she must understand fully why I must go back. He lifted her chin up and looked into her eyes.

"Quinna, I do not want to go, I do not enjoy the killing. There is really one reason why I feel I must go out again and soon—I am afraid if I do not lead another strike the braves will drift off. They are looking for a reason to go home. And if we stop now, we are finished as a people. We can not let up."

So that was it, she thought; it is not just revenge that motivates him, it is fear as well. She fingered the amulet that hung from her neck, saying a prayer to her guardian the hawk god. Ochala had made the bone amulet and carved the hawk into it to protect her. Maybe her guardian would watch over Tamoset also.

"It is good you and I met," she said, smiling now. "It must have been planned by the Great Spirit to help us get through these bad times. You are back to old Tamoset, the man I first met by the river. I remember when I got back to the village, the children told me about how they were scared of the man with the scar. But the ones who were in the planting fields spoke up and said no, he is not to be feared, he is good. They explained how you shot the groundhog and talked with them."

"I remember too. Mostly I remember seeing you by the river." He smiled at the thought. "I rubbed my eyes; I could not believe what I was seeing—I could not turn away."

"Yes, I know. And I was so mad, so embarrassed."

He gently pulled her backward, and they lay on the ground.

"That happened at a place very much like this; the river, the warm air, even a waterfall."

She kissed him, slowly.

He responded by holding her tight, then let his fingertips slide up and down her back, caressing the silky skin. He stopped kissing to look at her face, still overwhelmed by such beauty. Through the trees a dappled light fell on her, making her moist eyes shine.

She rolled on top, fitting her body snugly against his. She gave a low moan of pleasure, could not believe the power of this man, the intensity of her feeling toward him. She looked into his eyes, and whispered, "Don't ever leave me; whatever happens, we stay together."

"Together," he murmered.

Her eyes closed, and she let the happiness of love sweep over her.

Chapter 32

"Tamoset, can you hear me! Tamoset!"

Tamoset opened his eyes, looked up at the trees. Quinna lay sleeping beside him, the waterfall splashing nearby. He propped himself up, unsure if the distant calling he heard was in his dreams or was real.

"Tamoset, it is Apponac!" Apponac was a boy of twelve whom Tamoset had taken under his wing when the boy's parents died at the Great Swamp.

Tamoset stood.

"Over here, by the stream!" he shouted, in a gravelly voice.

Apponac dashed through the brush and burst into the opening by the waterfall. Quinna sat up and covered herself, alarmed at the intrusion.

"Why do you come here?" Tamoset said harshly.

"I've been looking all over for you. Come quick. Terrible news. Philip wants you."

"What's happened?"

"The camp by the Great River, it's been attacked. Many killed."

Quinna sprang up. "Where are the survivors? Are they here? What do you know of my relatives?"

"I don't know any more. A runner just came and told us of the attack. All the people are afraid; they think the whites will come to Wachusett next."

Without a word, Tamoset grabbed the sleeping baby and started running toward the camp. Quinna and Apponac followed.

At Wachusett he went straight to Philip's wigwam, expecting to find him outside holding council. But it was strangely quiet. He poked his head inside. It took a second for his eyes to adjust to the darkness. In the back of the wigwam Philip sat alone. Tamoset went in, asking, "What happened?"

Philip did not move. A second passed. Then, "It is over."

"What do you mean?"

"We are finished."

Tamoset looked closely at his friend, afraid his mind was not right.

As if reading his thoughts, Philip said, "I can see the end clearly now. Without the camp to the west, we are finished. Even you will soon see the same outcome."

"What happened?"

"The English attacked the camp on the Great River. They came at sunrise."

"Where were our guards?"

"There were none," Philip said in a soft voice, shaking his head.

Tamoset thought it odd that his friend was not screaming with rage; he looked at him again. Philip's eyes were open, but he was staring into space. Tamoset knew his friend was looking into the future.

"How many survived?" asked Tamoset.

"A few; they will be coming soon." His voice was hollow.

A chill ran up Tamoset's spine. Philip had never acted this way before. He was a man of action, and now he sat quietly, not making plans, not mentioning revenge.

The news was so bad, Tamoset closed his eyes, the shock and anger making him feel sick. Seconds later he asked, "Who did this to us? Ben Church?"

"No, the soldier they called Turner. He is dead, though; braves caught his men as they ran from the slaughter."

Then it dawned on Tamoset—Philip's wife and son were at that camp.

"Your wife and son?"

"No word."

They sat together quietly. Outside, they could hear the wailing; many had lost family members in the attack.

Finally Tamoset said, "It is not over. We still have braves here, good men who will fight."

"They will scatter like dust now. I have felt their resolve growing weak even before this."

So he senses it, too, thought Tamoset.

"Maybe not. I will organize a raid. Many will want blood. The whites will pay."

"We will see. But the signs are bad. The Narragansetts will not stay. The Nipmucks are almost gone; hundreds died at the Great River."

Someone came to the wigwam, calling, "Philip."

Philip stood, and went toward the opening. As he passed Tamoset he put his hand on Tamoset's shoulder. In a low voice, he said, "I will go on the next raid with you."

Tamoset was left alone in the wigwam. He knew Philip would hold the council; maybe once again he could rally his people. Minutes passed, and Tamoset thought of the Great River camp, could picture it in ashes, could see the dead being picked at by vultures and crows. The soldiers had come at dawn, he thought; they are learning, they are not afraid.

Finally he stood. It was evening now. He would speak at the council, speak for war, tell the people they were still strong, that soon the whites would tire and ask for peace. He did not believe this, but knew there was no option except to fight, and fight to the last man.

* * * *

The council had gone better than he expected; the braves were bent on revenge, ready to take to the warpath. Philip spoke eloquently, of how the whites attack camps of sleeping women and children, how the cowards must pay. All agreed that daring action must now be taken, and Boston itself must be attacked.

When Tamoset told Quinna he would be leaving in two or three days to lead the raid, she voiced her opposition, certain that his war party would be wiped out by the hordes of whites that inhabited Boston. He snapped at her, saying, "And what would you want us to do? Stay here and meet the same fate as the camp at the Great River?"

Quinna came right back at him. "A wise leader spares his men from battles they cannot hope to win. We should flee this country; it is cursed now anyway."

Tamoset stormed out, going to the edge of the camp to chip arrowheads. Once seated he thought about just how many warriors might be left. Perhaps 100 Wampanoags, 200 Nipmucks and 500 Narragansetts. We must attack at night, and must make sure we hit and run. We cannot continue to lose men charging garrisons. With each flick of his wrist he thought of the Bostonians who would die as the stone flakes flew.

Apponac ran up to him.

"Philip has decided to trade the white woman captive for the shiny metal," said the boy excitedly. "Her master has agreed. Word was sent to the English."

Tamoset wondered about this strategy. On the one hand, the natives could use the shillings to buy muskets from the French to the north. But he worried that somehow through negotiations the English might pinpoint the location of the camp. Surely they already know we are somewhere near Wachusett, he thought, but why risk letting them know the exact location for a few shillings?

Later in the morning the boy returned again, telling him that another runner from the west had arrived with more details from the Great River Camp. Philip's wife and son were alive. They had not been at the camp by the Falls, but to the north at another site on the river. They and a small party of other Wampanoags were in the process of trudging eastward and would arrive in a day or two.

When twenty arrowheads were made, Tamoset walked back to the center of camp. He would tell Philip that they should hit Boston immediately. On the way he saw a Narragansett woman outside her wigwam with a full basket strapped to her back. Her husband was packing his own basket.

Tamoset knew the man, and he stopped to watch. The man saw him but said nothing. When his basket was full he swung it onto his back, and the two walked away, heading toward the southern trail. A bad sign, thought Tamoset; they are leaving, going on their own, probably heading toward their tribal lands. He wanted to scream at them, wanted to tell them that surely they would be captured by the English, put on the white man's canoes to an unknown fate. Instead, he said nothing, watching them go, silently asking the Creator to guide their journey.

Chapter 33

Mary Rowlandson followed Tamoset out of the camp, nervous with hope. She could not believe that by the end of the day she might be free. Looking down at her feet, she thought how odd she would seem now to her fellow colonists. Her shoes had long since given out, and she wore ankle-high moccasins along with what remained of her black dress.

Behind her were five more braves and Apponac, who had improved his English by asking so many questions. She knew the price of her ransom was twenty pounds because that's what she suggested to her captors when they asked what the English might pay for her. A shrewd woman, she thought that if she said a lower amount the Indians might not think it worthwhile to let her go.

Apponac told her the English had agreed to the price and were sending a man to a place called Flat Rock to escort Rowlandson out of the forest. The man's name was John Hoar. The English said that if he were harmed, the the practice of trading captives for supplies or money would cease. Still, Hoar was either a very brave man or a fool.

Tamoset's role in the release was to oversee the transaction, but more importantly he was to make sure that no other Englishmen had followed Hoar to Flat Rock. He had selected four of the best braves to accompany him, and Apponac was to act as interpreter.

Now, as they approached the rock, Tamoset ordered Rowlandson to be seated just off the trail. He ordered Apponac and a brave to stay with her, while he and the others split into two groups, each making a wide arc around the rock to check for signs of English.

As he carefully surveyed the woods, stepping softly as a lynx through thick brush, Tamoset let his mind roam over the events of the last couple of days.

He had moved into Quinna's wigwam, but the magic of the first night and the day by the falls had disappeared; the tension of his upcoming departure for the Boston raid hung over them, choking the relationship.

In his heart, he knew she was right, that in all probability the mission was doomed. But still, the lure of attacking such a concentration of whites—like snakes in the den—was too much for him to ignore. He would go, and hopefully she would be there for him if and when he returned.

Tamoset and the brave picked their way through the forest, careful not to step on any fallen twigs. Birds were calling on the warm May day. A good sign, he thought; there are no intruders hiding nearby. Yet there was a part of him that wanted the whites to be there. This ransom business seemed wrong—why sell white women so they could have more babies to cover the land?

When they met the other two braves at the completion of their scouting circle, he instructed them to take up positions in the woods and watch for the arrival of the white man. If the Englishman was with others, they were to kill them all.

Tamoset went back to Rowlandson, and with Apponac and the warrior guard, they took her to Flat Rock, climbing to the top to better survey the area. He sat down, noting that the trees were fully leafed—soon it would be the moon of peas and shad. Almost a whole cycle of earth seasons had passed since the war started. He remembered that fateful first war council with Philip and how he screamed for war. Yes, he thought, I too wanted this, it was not just Philip. I must talk to him again and ask if he regrets the decision.

He glanced at Rowlandson; she was reading her bible. Do her gods live in paper, he wondered? Maybe so—after all, she was still alive, and soon might be free.

Rowlandson shifted, uncomfortable knowing the scar-faced Indian was watching her again. To her, he seemed like a wounded bear ready to explode at any minute. What does Quinna see in him? she asked herself.

Before the horse came in view, Tamoset knew it was coming—first he heard it, then he smelled it. Horse and rider entered the tiny clearing by the rock. Tamoset stood looking down at the mounted white man. He could hear Rowlandson weeping uncontrollably behind him, the first free white man she had seen in weeks.

Every fiber in Tamoset screamed to kill this man, wipe him off the face of the earth so he and his kind could do no more harm. He trembled with rage fighting to control himself.

Apponac, knowing Tamoset as he did, could see what was happening, and he worried that Tamoset might leap from the rock and onto the man.

"Are you Hoar?" asked Apponac, moving next to Tamoset.

"Yes."

"Do you have the shillings?"

Hoar dismounted. He reached into his coat and withdrew the money.

Tamoset leaned to Apponac, "Tell him to bring it here."

Apponac did as he was told. "Bring it up to us."

Hoar began walking up the hill alongside the rock, wondering if these would be the last steps he ever took. It would be a simple thing for the Indians to kill him, take the money and still keep Rowlandson.

At the top of the rock, Hoar was face to face with Tamoset. He could see the scar clearly now, knew this was the Indian he had been hearing about, the Indian that had led so many recent raids. His fear mounted; it was said this warrior was like a ghost, running through musket balls with no harm.

Apponac took the pouch of money from Hoar and began to count. It was all there, he told Tamoset.

Tamoset looked at Mary Rowlandson then back at Hoar. The white man's scent was strong and foul. It would be easy to kill him, he thought; his horse could feed many of our people. We gave our word to do no harm, but did the whites keep there word?

Apponac stood unmoving; with each passing second his anxiety increased. He knew Tamoset did not like this plan, knew his friend was now reconsidering. He looked at Hoar, could see the sweat on the man's brow—it was clear the white man knew what peril he was in.

Rowlandson broke the silence. "He has brought the money, now I am free," she said boldly, mustering her courage for the scar-faced Indian. But she did not rise.

Tamoset looked at her. He thought of Quinna saying how Rowlandson had courage, how she made herself useful by sewing items of clothing for the tribe.

Without saying a word, Tamoset jerked his head, indicating Rowlandson could go.

* * * *

Back at the camp, Tamoset went directly to Philip, who was sitting outside his wigwam talking to a Narragansett warrior. The Narragansett greeted Tamoset, then left.

"Is the white woman gone?" asked Philip.

"Yes, it went just as planned; here are the English coins."

Philip took the pouch without looking inside and stuffed it behind his wide belt of wampum.

"Sit for a moment, I have something to tell you," said Philip, packing a soapstone pipe with tobacco mixed with tiny shreds of tree bark. He smoked now to ease the hunger rather than for pleasure.

Tamoset sat, mentally exhausted from his personal struggle over whether or not to kill the white man Hoar.

Philip passed him the pipe; then in a hollow voice said, "I am going back to Montaup."

Tamoset looked at his friend, somehow not surprised by his decision. "And Boston?"

"Not enough warriors. The Narragansetts want to go south; they say there may be more warriors there."

"Is that what you think?"

"I don't know. It does not matter. We cannot stay here."

"Yes, we must leave Wachusett, but there are no warriors to the south, only tired Narragansetts who hide in the woods. If we go there, we can expect little help."

"That may be. But if I'm to die it should happen there."

Tamoset knew, without Philip saying it, that a battle in the homeland was the right thing to do.

Philip looked directly at his friend for the first time. "You are free now."

Tamoset looked at him quizzically, not understanding.

Philip drew on the pipe, let the blue-gray smoke settle deep into his lungs, then slowly released it through his nose. "You have done all you can. You have been my best warrior."

Tamoset felt uncomfortable. This talk was not like Philip; surely he was not finished with this war. "We have many raids to go on; with fewer braves we can hit like the wind."

"Yes, I am not done fighting. But you should go while you can, you have Quinna now, you have Chusett."

"And you have your family back also."

"But I started the war, and I must finish it."

A long silence, both men looking away. Then Tamoset shook his head. He drew his knife from his belt and used it to draw in the dirt. "Plymouth here," he said pointing, "Taunton here, let us hit them both."

A slow smile spread across Philip's face, and he thought, he's a warrior to the end. A true Wampanoag. Yes, one more chance to strike at the people he hated most: the whites of Plymouth, descendents of the first English boat, the ones my father Massasoit helped. It is only fitting that we burn that town or die trying. He put his hand on Tamoset's shoulder, "We go together."

Chapter 34

The tavern had a raw, musty smell, a place where fresh air rarely mingled with the business of eating and drinking. Each of the five rough pine tables had its own candle, but the place was still dark, especially now that the massive fireplace was idle on this warm July night.

John Homer and Ben Church were talking in a dim corner, the ale loosening their tongues and assisting the friendship between the two.

"So what did you do come nightfall?" asked Church, fascinated by Homer's story about hiding from the Indians after the surprise attack on the Connecticut River camp.

"It was awful. In fact, you're the first person I've told the story to. Up till now I just wanted to forget the whole nightmare."

Homer paused, taking a long drink of ale. He continued, "I could still hear screaming from the men the Indians had captured. I think they were torturing them one by one right there where they ambushed us by the stream."

"From what I hear," said Church, looking into his mug of ale, "it's a wonder anybody got out of there alive. Captain Holyoke is credited with saving the lives of many men after Turner was killed."

"Yes, he's a good man, plenty of courage. But when the Indians ambushed us, I lost sight of him altogether. He may have saved others, but for me it was the Praying Indian who saved my hide."

Homer packed his pipe, talking as he used the candle to light it. "Anyway, I was frozen with fear. Even though it was dark, I could tell the Indians were very close; I could hear them howling. They were in a rage; many had lost wives and children at the Falls."

Church interrupted, "Had to be done. You boys attacked at dawn; no way you could tell braves from squaws."

Homer nodded; he had fired his musket at anything that moved that morning and felt no remorse. He continued with the tale of his escape,

"I lay in that brush half the night. Finally, I realized the Indians might stay around into the next morning, and then I'd be a goner for sure. So I got my courage up and started creeping away from the savages and toward the big river. Once there I just slipped into the water and let the current carry me. I was too scared to swim for fear they might see me, so I just floated for what seemed like most of the night. At dawn I got out and started walking south. It was terrible going; I didn't dare use the paths."

"You did the right thing. Some of the men who got separated from the main company have not been heard from since. My guess is they were caught on the trail. "

A big, burly man entered the tavern, started toward the bar, but as his eyes grew accustomed to the dark, he spotted

Church. "Ben, you old scoundrel, I didn't know you was back in Plymouth!" he bellowed, coming toward the table.

"Good to see you, David; just here for a couple days organizing a group to go after King Philip himself. David Sawin, I want you to meet John Homer."

As the men shook hands Church continued, "John's coming with me to try and get the Sakkonets to join us."

"Aye, that will help the struggle. You've been right all along, Ben; the friendly Indians can make a difference; too bad it took the fools in power a year to figure that out."

"Never too late," said Church with a smile. "Sit down and join us."

Sawin slid a chair over while Church motioned for the tavern keeper to bring another tankard of ale. When the ale arrived, Sawin drank it without stopping, some spilling down his chin.

"Another tankard, friend, 'tis good for the spirit," he said to the tavern keeper, who knew that Sawin always drank his first ale in this fashion.

"Have you boys heard the story of Mary Rowlandson?" asked Sawin, scratching his thick, red beard.

Homer shook his head no, and Church said, "Only bits and pieces. What hear you, David?"

"Well we all know that Philip is coming southward—if he isn't here already—but this Rowlandson woman was captive for months with Philip himself. She says some of the Narragansetts were running off even while still at Wachusett."

Church raised a hand, then he pounded the table. "Every time I hear the mention of the Wachusett Camp, I get so mad.

We should have hit them there. It would not have been hard to find the camp; then we could have had one big battle to end this thing. Now the devils are on the move, harder than ever to find."

"And they will be in their homeland," added Homer. "I don't relish the thought of fighting them in a swamp again like the first time."

"You're right, John," said Church. "All the more reason I appreciate your coming here. When I wrote to you and asked you to join me in the field again I didn't think you would really come."

"Got to end this thing," said Homer quietly. "They killed my son."

"Sorry to hear that," said Sawin, looking into his ale.

After an awkward silence, Church said, "What else did Mrs. Rowlandson have to say?"

"She said plenty. Had a dreadful time of it, poor woman. Couple of her children died, she herself was close to starving before an Indian woman took pity on her and shared her food. And listen to this. She said that old Philip himself treated her kindly, much more so than the rest of the heathens. How do you figure?"

Church ran his fingers back through his hair, a frown on his face. "'Tis a curious thing. Philip is part devil, that's for sure—yet there is more to the man. To have been this successful for so long, he must be a smart one. And I've talked to settlers that knew him before the war, they say he had a dignity about him, even offered them advice on where to hunt."

"Well," said Sawin, "I heard me all sorts of stories about the red king. I figured most were untrue, figured he was just a filthy beast. But I've got to believe Mrs. Rowlandson, she was with him, even knitted his son a cap. They say she also was with the scarface Indian, the one that leads the raids. Why just last—"

"What? An Indian with a scar?" asked Homer, sitting up straight.

"What's the matter, John?" said Church. "You've seen this Indian?"

"More than once, more than once. Can't hardly believe he's still alive."

"Well," said Sawin, "she said he was quite alive and lookin' meaner than ever. Said she thought he was going to kill her just seconds before her release."

"Did she talk about any other Indians," asked Church, "Matoonas or the one they call Muttawmp?"

"Didn't mention neither, but I know for a fact Matoonas is dead. He was captured just three days ago. From what I hear, his head sits on a pole in the middle of Boston's common."

"Certainly got them on the run, but it's a long way from over, can't let them catch their breath," said Church. "Listen, it's getting late. John and I leave in two days for the Elsabeths by Cape Cod. We're going to have two Nausets paddle us along the shore toward Sakkonet country. When we get back, we sure would like to have you join us when we search for Philip."

Sawin heaved his huge frame out of the chair. "As long as your leadin' the men, Ben. I'm not goin' out with some Bostonian lookin' to make a name for himself." Then as an afterthought, "Wouldn't mind pickin up some land for myself, that Montaup area is good growin' country."

The men shook hands, agreeing to meet in ten days.

* * * *

A light breeze blew from the west, but the two Indian paddlers held the canoe on a perfect course, always maintaining at least a hundred yards between themselves and the shore. Church had made it clear that to go closer might put them in arrow range—he didn't really know what to expect from the Sakkonets. For that matter, Philip himself could be anywhere in the vicinity, and Church wasn't about to take any chances with just Homer to aid him.

Church chatted with the paddlers in their native tongue, asking about various Indian leaders, talking as if he were out on a duck hunt. The Nausets had stayed out of the war, and Church had used their services frequently.

Homer kept a wary eye on the coastline. How can Church be so relaxed, he wondered? Can't see three feet beyond all that greenery; a whole war party could be hiding behind it. Worse, they might have canoes of their own.

In spite of his unease, Homer would rather be traveling by water than by land. He had developed a case of claustrophobia after spending the night alone in the woods near the Connecticut River. The lushness of the vegetation and the thickness of the brush made his escape a nightmare—always thinking a warrior would rise out of the forest in front of him.

He was weary of fighting, and tired of being away from his wife. And although he hadn't said anything to Church, his stomach was in a constant knot, his fear was so great. But after watching his son die, Homer had sworn he would stay with the battle until it was over. It took all his will to keep the promise.

"This is great country down here, John," remarked Church, taking in a deep breath of salt air. "Good soil, and the growing season lasts longer because it's close to the ocean. And, oh, the fish. Eels, striped bass, flatfish, shellfish, alewives—no wonder Philip fights for the land."

"Do you think he'd ever give up?"

"You mean surrender? Not on your life. He knows he'd be beheaded or hanged. You know what Philip told Roger Williams before the war? He said, 'I am determined not to live until I have no country.' Now I know he's my enemy, and I hate what the savages have done, but you have to have respect for a man that says that and then does something about it."

Homer didn't answer. Church was a tough one to figure out. He's killed more Indians than any white man, Homer mused, but yet he talks fondly of them.

"Yes," continued Church. "Got to respect him. And some of these friendly Indians, like these two," Church waved his hand at the two paddlers, "are better people than half the settlers I know. If you treat them fairly they will do the same. 'Tis a sad—Look!"

Church pointed to a rocky point ahead. Indians were fishing, and none had as of yet noticed the oncoming canoe.

Butterflies danced in Homer's stomach. All his past missions had been with large numbers of troops. Now, he thought, I am in a canoe with just one other white man, and there are at least twenty Indians ahead. He picked his musket off the floor of the canoe.

"Easy, John. Put that thing back. Remember why we're here. Got to see if they want to talk."

"But how do you know they're Sakkonets?"

"I don't. Reckon we're going to find out a mite quick."

Church let out a loud halloo. The natives on the rocks scrambled to their feet, shocked to see a canoe with white men coming at them.

"Go closer," said Church to the paddlers.

Homer gripped the canoe sides, thinking that if not for his faith in Church's knowledge of the enemy, he would have picked up his musket and ordered the paddlers to race away.

The natives on the rocks were now gesturing for them to come ashore. They were shouting, but Church could not understand them above the surf.

"John, I need to talk with them a bit, but not here. Can't hear a thing. Look at all those trees behind them; could be more hiding in there. I'm going to motion for them to follow us along the shore; there's a place up ahead that's open."

Church waved the natives ahead, and two of the swiftest ran along the shore keeping up with the canoe.

"Ben," said Homer nervously, "I think we best make them swim out to us and do your talking from the canoe."

Church laughed, "They won't come out here. How do they know we won't kill them? No, I've got to go to them; it's us that needs their help."

When they came to the opening, Church shouted in the native tongue, "I've come to talk to Awashonks. She knows me, Benjamin Church. We were friends."

"Yes, Yes, come. We will take you to her."

Church was nervous now. He figured his odds were little better than even of surviving the day. He cupped his hand and shouted back, "Put your bows far down the beach; then when you return I will come ashore. Stand back from the water a little. My men in the boat will be watching. If any harm comes to me, all the English will know the Sakkonets are the enemy."

The two Sakkonets did as they were told and returned to the open area. Church surveyed the area one last time and instructed the paddlers to bring him in. Then he leaned toward Homer and said, "Stay in the canoe and watch for my return. I may not be back until nightfall. If I don't return, go back to Plymouth and tell the others what happened."

"Ben, are you sure you want to do this? We could ask them to bring Queen Awashonks here. You could negotiate right on this beach."

"I'll be fine, God willing." The canoe was within a few feet of where the little waves broke. Church put one leg over, then the other and slogged to shore. He turned back to Homer and with a wave of his hand said, "See you at dusk."

Homer watched him greet the two natives; then the three men disappeared into the green, jungle-like forest.

* * * *

The western sky was streaked with pinks and darker shades of crimson. Ducks winged their way back and forth along the shoreline, their calls echoing off the water.

In the bobbing dugout canoe, Homer's back ached. How did the paddlers remain so still? he wondered. Do they feel no discomfort? The two Nausets knew a little English and Homer talked to them, asking their opinions about the chances for peace. One of them said, "Until Philip dead, only blood."

Homer thought that just about summed it up. We may have the natives on their heels, but Philip has proven more than once he could bounce back. He recalled how at the outset of the war the English thought they had Philip trapped in the Pocasset Swamp and that the fight would be over in a matter of weeks.

Suddenly, just as the last bit of light left the sky, warriors appeared on the shore. They stood there, armed with bows and lances, pointing out at the canoe. At any second Homer expected Church to step from the woods and wave that all was fine. But minutes passed, and there was no sign of him, just the natives who were talking excitedly and gesturing toward the canoe.

Homer looked at his musket lying at his feet—it would do little good against so many natives. Still, he was inclined to load it, if only for the security it furnished. He glanced at his two paddlers, stoic faces showing nothing, but eyes scanning the horizon for other canoes. One of them said, "Could be trick. Maybe canoe full of Indians coming."

"Damn," Homer muttered, "where is Church?" He felt totally helpless. To go ashore would be folly; yet, to remain drifting offshore made them sitting ducks for a surprise attack from swifter canoes. He turned to one of the paddlers, saying, "Ask them where Church is." The man shouted out the question.

Those on shore looked at each other, then one started laughing. He said something to the others, and all laughed and pointed into the woods. Then he cupped his hands and shouted toward the canoe.

Homer looked at the paddler nearest him, waiting for the translation.

The paddler looked grim, and said, "He say if white man come ashore he must be looking for his scalp."

Homer weighed his options, none of them good. He could head back to Plymouth before natives came after them in canoes, or he could wait longer. Maybe if we mention Awashonks' name, he thought, they will know we mean no harm. "Tell them we are friends of Awashonks, and that one of our men is with her now."

When the natives on shore heard that, they nodded, waved and melted back into the woods. Homer watched, wondering if they knew more than they were saying; maybe Church was already dead. He figured his own odds of escaping the night without being attacked were lessoning with each hour. "Paddle out a little farther, we are too close," he commanded tersely.

The evening turned to night, and blackness engulfed the canoe. The shore was only visible by looking at where the treetops met the sky—that was where the stars ended. Homer was grateful there was no wind, but still, another canoe could sneak quite close before it was detected. He spent his time searching the blackness for any shadow on the water, all the time expecting a war whoop to shatter the silence.

Finally, one of the paddlers said, "Me no like it very much. Ben Church must be dead man. We go home now or we all die."

"No," hissed Homer, "not yet."

The man glared at him, and Homer wondered if the paddler might just turn on him. He glanced at his musket, not knowing in the dark that the man did the same. Homer struggled to remain calm. Then he said flatly, "Ben Church not dead, wait until dawn."

An uneasy silence settled over the canoe. Homer's back was in agony and he longed to lie down, but didn't dare. He thought there was a good chance the paddlers would club him while he slept. So he sat, looking toward shore, wondering what he would tell Church's wife if his friend did not return.

A couple hours later he thought he saw a light in the forest. Raising himself on his knees he craned his neck up, asking, "Light, did you see light?"

The paddler with whom he had argued earlier said. "Yes, me see light, could be trouble."

Homer stared into the blackness. "There, I saw it again."

Through the trees an orange glow flickered, getting closer, stronger, until finally it was on the beach. Someone was standing there holding a torch, others were around him. Homer held his breath. Then a shout came over the water, "John, it's Ben! All right to come in now!"

Homer broke into a smile, letting out a deep sigh. "Let's go, but slowly, got to get a good look at them." He worried that maybe Church was made to halloo them under knifepoint.

As they paddled closer it was clear all was well; Church was shaking the hand of a tall native woman. Must be Awashonks, thought Homer.

Church was waiting for them. He said something over his shoulder to Awashonks and then waded out to the canoe. Once inside he slapped Homer on the back. "Sorry I took so long. They had a big fire, and each chief had to dance and show his loyalty."

"I thought you was dead," said Homer in the dark, "I really did. Some Indians came to the shore and they didn't look none to friendly."

"Don't know who those were, but all is well. Couple tense moments when I first got to Awashonks' village. One of the lesser chiefs even raised his tomahawk and started coming toward me. If not for the Queen I'd have lost my hair to be sure."

"So she's joining us?"

"Yup, and she's got quite a few warriors. Told her we would meet back here in ten days; then we can start the hunt for Philip. They say he's no more than twenty miles from here."

Chapter 35

Tamoset breathed deeply of the salt air; the scent brought back a flood of memories. He thought of earlier times when he and Napatoo would walk the shore, digging clams and shooting ducks. It was strange to be back in the homeland, hiding in a place where once life was so free.

Quinna was behind him in the long line of what was left of Philip's followers. She too smelled the ocean, saying, "I would like to see the great water again; it is more amazing than I imagined."

Tamoset shifted the pack which carried Chusett. He was light-headed from hunger, could barely wait until camp was made where they would roast the striped bass caught at the shore. "Yes, it is beautiful. And when the Creator is angry, it is a wild thing to see."

"How much farther will we go before resting?"

"Philip did not say. We must move often; it is wise not to stay in one camp for long. The whites are everywhere. It makes me sick to see more of our land plowed than before."

"But we cannot walk every day." Quinna was exhausted from many days of walking on lesser trails. She wondered when Philip would realize the futility of the fight.

"No," sighed Tamoset, wiping sweat from his brow. "Once a safe place is found for the women and children, the warriors

will go off and attack the coastal towns. Word of our raids will
reach the Narragansetts hiding to the south, and they will take
courage. Maybe they will join us once more."

He thought of telling her again that she should take
Chusett and go north. The Abenakis would welcome them; the
French would look the other way. But they had argued long
and bitterly over this before. She would not leave him now,
could not leave him to an unknown fate. She had said,
"Whatever happens, happens to us together."

And so they stayed with Philip as the others did, including
Philip's own wife and child. The entire group consisted of
roughly seventy-five followers, and this was their tenth day
scavenging through the woods along the coastal area near Montaup.

They walked all day, the July sun pounding down on the
procession, their progress slowing as the heat increased. Finally,
when the crickets began to sing and the whipporwill to call,
Philip halted the column by a clear-flowing stream. The women
set up racks to smoke the fish, and the men rested with their
pipes.

Philip, Tamoset and two other warriors sat together smoking and talking about where to go next. Tamoset wanted to attack Dartmouth immediately, but Philip wanted to raid an
outpost at Bridgewater. The two other men thought they
should go to their old village at Montaup, thinking they might
find some hidden corn that the whites had overlooked.

Suddenly a scout who had been instructed to follow the
main party at some distance ran into camp. He was out of
breath, but when he saw Philip he broke into a big smile and

stammered, "You were right. The English are hunting for us. There is a group just to the east."

Philip snapped, "Why not the face of a warrior?" referring to his smile.

"Only fifteen English and one native. All armed with muskets. They will be easy to kill; then we have muskets."

"Who is the native?"

"I was too far away to be sure, but it looked like one of us."

Tamoset and Philip exchanged glances, incredulous that a Wampanoag could be guiding the whites.

"I think we should go after them," said one of the warriors.

Philip turned to Tamoset, "What do you think?"

Tamoset paused, weighing the possible consequences of turning back to attack. The women and children would have to wait here, certainly not the best hiding place. On the other hand, they had not drawn white blood in some time—the warrior spirit might be leaving some of the men. And the muskets would be invaluable.

"We should kill them," he said flatly.

"Then we will go," said Philip getting to his feet. "Be ready when I call. I'll have my wife pack the fish; we can eat on the trail."

Tamoset went back to Quinna, explaining the decision. Without a word she brought out her paint bags and started mixing the colored powder with a bit of bear grease. When it was ready Tamoset covered his face in red paint, then smeared streaks of yellow down his cheeks and across his chest.

As he stood to leave Quinna grabbed his hand and pulled herself up. Her eyes were moist.

"Go with the eagle, be like the fox," she whispered hoarsely. It was an old Nipmuck saying for departing warriors.

"Yes. Do not worry. I have always come back, haven't I?"

"Just remember me, remember your son."

He knew she was reminding him not to take unnecessary risks. He stroked her cheek, then wheeled away, trotting back to where Philip was waiting with the others.

Philip picked ten warriors, five of them only boys, to remain and guard the women. Tamoset saw the disappointment on their faces, so eager were they for the fight. But other boys were allowed to accompany the thirty men who were going after the English, and he heard one of them say, "Finally, I am a warrrior." Tamoset winced; they had no idea of the hardship of the warpath. But we need them, he thought. We might be in for a bad fight.

Philip led the war party out of camp at a trot to the east. He would give the whites what they were searching for.

* * * *

The moon guided the war party's steps along the path. When they had traveled roughly seven miles, Philip had them slow to a walk, with wide spaces between each man.

"Tamoset," said Philip softly, "you have night eyes; lead the way with me."

Together they carefully picked their way along the trail, careful to step over fallen twigs and branches. Even in the dark they could feel the twigs through their thin moccasins, knowing to avoid putting their weight there. They stopped often, all standing motionless and listening for any unusual noise. Under the moon they were like wolves, silently stalking their prey. They continued on, arrows already notched in the bows.

Tamoset abruptly raised his arm, signaling all to halt. Ahead through the trees was a dim glow. A campfire. Philip saw it too.

He hissed in Tamoset's ear, "Not Ben Church; he never allows fires."

Tamoset nodded, motioning for the braves to spread out around the perimeter of the camp. By prearrangement they knew to creep forward when they heard Philip give a single hoot of an owl. Three hoots meant attack.

Softly Tamoset said to Philip, "We must get the men close to the whites so they have no time to load their muskets. But they may have a guard posted, maybe two. Let's go and see."

Together they inched closer to the camp, pausing between each step, looking for unusual shadows by trees, figuring the guards would be leaning or sitting against the trunks. Then Philip slowly put his hand out, touching Tamoset lightly—a guard was up ahead.

The men stood motionless, scanning the woods for other guards. They used their ears and noses as well as their eyes. Maybe a guard would snap a twig, even light a pipe. Minutes went by, and they were about to go in on the lone guard when they heard a cough from their left. Tamoset pointed and slowly went toward the sound.

He did not make a direct path, instead letting his feet tell him where to step. Soon he spotted the shadowy outline of a man at the base of a tree. Tamoset thought about shooting an arrow, but he worried that the branches might deflect it, and even if he hit the man he might still cry out. So he carefully circled around behind the Englishman and slowly approached him from the rear. When he was just four feet away he drew his knife, then took the next two steps as if in slow motion. Now he was behind the tree.

In one quick motion he used his right hand to cover the Englishman's mouth while he used his other hand to slit the guard's throat. He felt the man jerk violently then slump, the blood warm and sticky on Tamoset's knife-holding hand. The Englishman was dead, never knowing what happened, never uttering a sound.

Tamoset went back to where he left Philip. He waited in the dark, watching the shadow of Philip rise up alongside the other guard and strike him with his stone hatchet. The Englishman grunted as he fell forward, and Philip froze. He stayed crouched next to the fallen Englishman, wondering if anyone in the slumbering camp had heard. He let a couple minutes pass, then returned to Tamoset, confident that the English were unaware of the fate of the guards.

In the darkness the two men nodded at each other, then Philip gave one long hoot. Braves inched their way closer, some not stopping until they were thirty feet from the English fire. Tamoset waited, heart pounding. Even though he had been in dozens of battles, the adrenaline coursed through his body, making him high with a mixture of fear and excitement. The whites would pay, his mind screamed, pay for trying to track us like animals.

Philip lifted his hands to his mouth again, slowly, clearly hooting three times. The woods exploded with blood-chilling shrieks as the warriors charged the camp, tomahawks raised.

A few Englishmen managed to stumble to their feet before the warriors were on them, others never making it out of their bedrolls. Tamoset charged with the others, but out of the corner of his eye he saw someone run from the camp, and he gave chase.

The Englishman went wildly crashing through the woods, Tamoset gaining with each step. When he was within five feet he hurled himself onto the back of the fleeing man and they went crashing into the brush. In the darkness Tamoset easily overpowered his enemy, quickly realizing it was not a man but a boy, weighing little more than a hundred pounds.

With one hand he grabbed the boy's neck, pinning him to the ground, and raised his tomahawk with the other hand. Just then the moon emerged from behind a cloud and Tamoset could see the boy's terrified white face. His eyes were bugging out from lack of breath and both his hands were clawing at Tamoset's arm. A second passed, the boy's struggles growing weaker.

For the first time in the war, hesitation gripped Tamoset. This is my enemy, he thought, destroy him. He tightened his grip harder. But the hand that held the tomahawk did not move.

The moonlight faded again and the two were in total darkness. Suddenly Tamoset swung the tomahawk, burying it in the ground just an inch from the boy's head. He released the boy and watched him cough and hack, rolling to his side.

Tamoset stood. He could hear the screams of the dying white men behind him. He considered taking the boy captive, but what good would it do, he thought, we need to travel fast and a captive would just slow us and eventually be killed.

The boy lifted his head and with wild eyes stared at the dark shadow above him. He could not move with fear, could not call out.

When the boy didn't move Tamoset kicked him savagely. Now the boy scrambled to his feet and took off into the forest, branches crashing as he ran.

Tamoset went back to the camp. The fighting had stopped; Englishmen lay dead everywhere. Philip was crouched over a body, saw Tamoset approach and motioned for him to come.

Philip turned the bloodied head of the dead man toward him. Tamoset could see it was not an Englishman but a native, the white's scout.

"Look closely," snarled Philip.

Tamoset did so, turning the head to catch a bit more of the moonlight. Then he saw it. He knew this warrior. It was one of Awashonk's men. With disgust Tamoset dropped the head.

Philip stepped on the face of the dead man, grinding it into the ground. "He does not deserve to go to the other side." He looked at Tamoset, shaking his head, "It is hard for me to believe that now even Wampanoags turn against us. Awashonks will pay."

Chapter 36

They were too tired to run back to where the women and children waited, so they walked, the first hints of dawn showing to the east. Tamoset was next to Philip on the woodland trail. They had talked a bit at first, but now travelled in silence, each lost in his own gloomy thoughts.

Learning that Awashonks had turned against them came as a total surprise. It was a disaster. Her braves knew this country well, and it would only be a matter of time before more whites came, led by the very best of her warriors.

They passed a burned-out farmhouse and stopped to look among the charred timbers for useful items. Other braves picked through the adjacent field finding a few peas and beans that grew among the weeds. Hunger was as much an enemy as the soldiers—all the moving and all the hiding did not allow for time to plant.

They pushed on through the forest, looking forward to the sleep they had been deprived of to make the raid. As they approached the camp Tamoset noted how quiet it was; the women were doing a good job keeping the children's voices down.

Through the tunnel of green that flanked the trail he saw the little camp clearing ahead, saw someone sleeping, lying on the ground. Where were the guards, he thought, why don't they greet us? Something is wrong—no, no, his mind screamed. He ran forward, the others following.

Breaking into camp, they almost stepped on the bodies scattered about. Eight were dead from musket balls, three of them women. There were no signs of life. Tamoset was frantic. He started screaming for Quinna, but there was no answer. Not again, he pleaded silently, not again. Other braves knelt over the bodies, pounding the ground in desperation over the loss of loved ones.

Philip's face, contorted in rage, looked like that of a bull ready to charge. He turned to the braves, "More traitors!" he screamed, certain that only a native could have led the whites to such a secluded location.

"They will not see the end of this day alive!" He had his tomahawk in one hand, musket in the other, his knuckles white where he gripped them like a vise.

"Half of you come with me, we will find their trail! Tamoset, you and the others stay here, find those who have survived and move them further into the swamp." He spun around and dashed out, leaving the braves to decide quickly who would follow and who would stay.

Tamoset calmed himself, carefully walking around the edge of the camp, searching the vegetation for signs of disturbance. It was not easy finding the trail of the survivors. When the whites attacked, those that could escape scattered in all directions, only later regrouping and moving toward the swamp.

It took him two hours to find the main trail, and then half the day to finally reach the fleeing people. The first person he saw was Quinna, with Chusett safely on her back. They hugged, tears flowing, but there was no time to talk. Night was approaching and it was imperative to find a hidden resting spot.

As he led the group deep into the swamp, he knew that Philip's wife and son must have been taken prisoner. They were not among the survivors nor were they among the dead. He could only hope that Philip had overtaken the soldiers and freed them.

It wasn't until dark that they came upon a small island suitable for spending the night. With no wigwams, they were fortunate the sky was clear. Much of the shellfish and bass taken at the beach had been destroyed by the whites, but enough was saved for one last meal. Tomorrow they would have to scrounge for frogs, snakes, turtles and anything else they could put in the cooking pot.

He posted five guards around the edge of the camp; then he settled down next to Quinna on a deer-hide covering to talk. She told him of the surprise attack by the whites, confirming that they were led by natives.

"Did you see what happened to Philip's wife?" Tamoset asked.

"No, nothing. It happened so suddenly I only had time to grab Chusett and flee. The braves you left behind fought bravely; if not for them the whites would have killed us all."

"I should have known this would happen. Three days ago I was awake at dawn and saw an owl glide through the camp. I chose to ignore the omen, never telling anyone."

"The signs are confusing." She hesitated, then decided to continue.

"I have not told you about my dream. I've had it twice. In it, Philip is powerful again, he is so strong he fights and destroys the English by himself. It was a strange dream, and I thought about it often, wondering what it means. You are not in the dream; Philip fights alone."

Tamoset shook his head; the dream was wrong. He could not abandon Philip, not now, not when so many others had turned against him. He knew that through his decision he was dooming Quinna and Chusett, for they would not leave without him.

We are in a spiderweb, he thought; we will all be killed because of our loyalty. Maybe this is how it is meant to be, maybe it's better than what life would be watching the whites expand. Then he looked at Chusett, his sleeping face starting to show thinness from lack of proper food.

"It is time for us to separate," he said in a soft voice, hoping she would reconsider. "Chusett won't make it unless you take him north."

"And I won't make it without you."

Tamoset rolled away from her and looked up through the branches at the black sky. He would not argue, did not know how many more days they had together. Never had he felt so trapped.

"Tamoset, listen to me, please. What do Chusett and I have without you? Ochala is gone; my people are scattered to the winds. How do you know it will be better to the north? The whites will come there, too. Together, we always have a chance. That is what I believe. Let us see what Philip decides when he returns; maybe now he will go north."

"Yes, maybe," Tamoset lied. He could not imagine Philip leaving, especially if he did not recover his wife and son.

"You are right about the whites; they will expand northward after they settle the Wampanoag and Nipmuck land. Land is why they hate us so; that is what they want. I should have killed that boy today, I—"

"What boy?"

"I did not tell you? I am tired, so tired I forget what I say. Last night when we raided the other English soldiers' camp, all the braves charged in, but I saw someone running out. I chased and caught him, and even in the dark I knew it was just a boy, he was so small. I raised my tomahawk to kill him, but did not, could not. I cannot explain it."

"I know—whether you realized it or not you thought of Chusett."

Tamoset was silent. Then he said, "Perhaps. Nothing is clear anymore."

* * * *

Philip found his way back to the group the next day. His wife and child were not with him. He spoke to no one, and no one spoke to him. He sat alone, beyond the others, by the edge of a slow, brown stream.

Braves came to Tamoset throughout the day, asking what Philip had decided. "I have not talked to him," he said. "He needs to be alone now; he will give us his counsel in time."

But the night passed, then another day and Philip stayed out by the stream. None of the warriors dared approach him.

Finally, Tamoset went. He went to put his hand on his friend's shoulder, but Philip knocked his arm away with a vi-

cious blow. "We should never have left them," he growled. "I
did not want to, but you and the others insisted we raid the
soldiers. Why did I listen to you? None of your counsel has
been wise."

Tamoset was stung. He stepped back and waited to see if
Philip said more. He was about to counter that no one could
have predicted what would happen, no one thought the women
and children were in any real danger. Instead he said nothing,
backing away from Philip, who did not turn his gaze from the
passing water.

Chapter 37

The air was so still and heavy that Homer could feel the moisture as he trudged along the trail. His shirt was soaked with perspiration and the musket on his shoulder dug into his flesh. Behind him, he could hear the labored breathing of David Sawin and knew the big man was having a tough go of it.

If Church hadn't mentioned how steady Sawin was under fire, he would have wondered why he was asked to join the expedition. The others were in top shape, from months of drilling and fighting under Church's command. It was a large group, almost a hundred men, a little more than half soldiers, and the rest warriors from Awashonks' tribe.

Up ahead Church raised his hand. Quickly word filtered back that there would be a fifteen-minute rest. Ever since a smaller group of soldiers had returned with Philip's wife and son three days earlier, Church had pushed the men hard, searching for Philip's hideout. With the aid of native allies he knew he was getting closer, knew that somewhere in the huge swamp were the last remnants of Philip's followers.

Homer shed his pack and sat on the trail, the humidity having sapped his strength. He drank greedily from his skin of water, then flopped back on the ground.

Sawin nudged him with his boot, "Looks like you just rested your weary bones in poison ivy," he said, trying to hide a smirk.

"Damn," muttered Homer, raising himself to the sitting position and glancing behind at vines of shiny green leaves. He looked at Sawin and felt like taking a swing at his smug face. He couldn't explain why, but he didn't trust the man and wished he would march next to someone else. He wished Church had never introduced him.

Sawin waved his hand at the mosquitoes that were gathering. "I hate this place. These redskins always head into the swamps. Satan himself wouldn't live here." Sawin maneuvered himself away from the poison ivy and lay back on pine needles and oak leaves.

Putting his hands behind his head, he said, "But it will all be worth it if we get King Philip; in fact maybe I'll be the one to kill him myself. There's sure to be a few shillings for the man that puts a musket ball in him. And then after, imagine the good farmland that'll open up. No more of these cursed swamps, just open fields and snug farmhouses. Yes sir, it's going to be a great country, and don't you forget it."

Homer was about to tell him to keep his thoughts to himself, but the men in front were rising to their feet. Apparently Church had given the order to resume the march.

Sawin grunted and rose. He hoisted his musket and laughed, "We're close now; that red king is running low on hiding places."

* * * *

In the heart of the night, Philip sat alone by the sluggish stream. Sleep would not come; when he closed his eyes he saw his wife, saw his son and he thought his heart would break.

Now, as he waited for dawn he thought of his father. He recalled the day Massasoit first took him to see the whites at Plymouth. He was just in his eighth summer, and the whites had not yet expanded beyond coastal areas. When he and Massasoit entered the village the whites all showed respect, greeting his father warmly. At first he was terrified of the whites with their ugly looks, broken teeth, and dark robes. But as their visit lengthened, and he saw how easy his father dealt with them, his fear lessened and he watched everything they did closely. He was amazed by their square houses, the shiny knives and pots and the long steel rods his father said made a sound like thunder and would injure like an arrow.

Philip shook his head, as if to clear the memory. Muskets, knives, pots—we've grown to need those things, he thought bitterly. We gave land for their foolish metal, and slowly we grew weak. Better to have taken nothing. Those things are how they took our spirit. If only Massasoit could have known.

He reached down and scooped up a handful of brown muck at his feet. He watched it ooze from his fingers. Earth. Soon I will come to you. And if I make it to the other side I will see Massasoit and tell him what I've done. I have no regrets. Better to have tried than to watch them slowly push our people back till we had nothing. Now I can die as a warrior. Now I can die with honor.

He thought about the many battles he had fought in. We did well. The whites would never have stopped us on their own. No, they used the weak among our people to lead them. They pit one tribe against another, and only the English win. I tried to explain that to the people, but we started too late; too many of us were corrupted.

As he went over the battles, he thought of how Tamoset had transformed from a reluctant advisor to his best warrior. Yes, Tamoset, you have been true. And what did I do to thank you? You must know that I spoke without wisdom, that I spoke from anger. You are not responsible for my sorrow; you have been a true warrior while others failed. You are a brother to me. Forgive me, my friend.

He did not notice that the sky had lightened until he heard crows calling in the distance. He looked, could not see the birds but wondered why the racket. Maybe they're mobbing a hawk. He kept his eyes toward the sound, but saw nothing in the sky. Something must be on the ground, he thought, the crows have seen something. Maybe soldiers.

He sprang to his feet, started to turn toward the sleeping camp, then stopped. Time for the others to flee without me. If I am gone, they will go north and live.

Grabbing his musket, powder horn and shot bag, he turned toward the sound of the crows and started moving rapidly that way. Adrenaline coursed through him—his exhaustion forgotten. He knew the enemy would not expect him to be coming right at them, and he hoped to kill at least one of them before their muskets turned on him.

He was closer now; he could hear the crows just up ahead. He slowed to a crouched walk. He noticed the trees, how vividly green and beautiful their color. Odd, he thought, I've never seen them look this way before. He wondered if it were his last look at this world. At least I am in the land of our people, it is right to die here. They never got my soul.

A flash of steel caught his eye. He saw the soldiers at the same time they saw him, and he dashed to his left, scrambling down a hill. He heard a shot, then the whine of a musket ball sail past. But he was distancing himself from the pursueing soldiers, leading them away from the camp. He knew the soldiers could not keep up with him. As he ran he felt a peace, even a joy, knowing he would fight again.

Then a twig snapped ahead and he saw a tall thin Englishman step from behind a tree and raise his musket. Next to the Englishman one of Awashonk's warriors did the same. Philip pivoted and raced through the swamp, water splashing, slowing him down.

He heard the boom, and was catapulted forward. He felt nothing but knew he was hit, knew he was falling, spinning. His father's face flashed before his eyes, then a great peace smothered him in light, and he fell face first into the water.

* * * *

The crack of the musket shots could clearly be heard in the camp, and Tamoset leapt to his feet, grabbing his bow. At the same time one of the guards came bursting into camp crying, "English! They killed Philip!"

Instantly Tamoset knew what Philip had done.

Quinna looked at him, clutching Chusett, her eyes wild with fear.

Tamoset hesitated, glancing toward the stream where Philip had been sitting alone. Then he shouted, "This way!" and he started running northward, away from the English, away from Montaup, away from Philip's body.

About the Author

Michael Tougias is the author of a number of books about New England:

- *New England Wild Places*
- *Autumn Trails*
- *Nature Walks in Eastern Massachusetts*
- *Nature Walks in Central and Western Massachusetts*
- *Country Roads of Massachusetts*
- *The Hidden Charles*
- *A Taunton River Journey*

Tougias gives narrated slide presentations for each of his books, including *Until I Have No Country*. If you are interested in his slide presentations or publications, please write to him at P.O. Box 72, Norfolk, MA 02056.